OFFSPRING.

The Descendants.

Short Stories

By R.M. Alwyn

CONTENTS.

PROLOGUE.

Thousands of years ago, extraterrestrial shapeshifters arrived on Earth and manipulated human evolution, ruling as gods. As time passed, the allure of attraction and pleasure began to tempt many. Driven by the instincts of their human and animal avatars, they sought companionship and had children. Some of these remarkable hybrids inherited many of their parents' capabilities. Ancient writings resonate with fables of gods seamlessly transforming into animals. In modern times, people view these tales as mere exaggerations, and they have faded with the passage of time. However, what history has forgotten, legend and folklore remember. Here lie those untold stories.

STORY ONE.

THE FALLEN OGRE.

Passage One.

Golden Sunsets.

Golden Sunsets and Deep Dark Caverns. At the western edge of the Shimane Peninsula lies Izumo, a place deeply entrenched in mystical lore. Here, enchanting landscapes of beaches and majestic headlands stretch into the sea, offering awe-inspiring vistas of the setting sun. Revered Shrines Stand proudly along this stretch of coastline; their ancient origins intricately woven into the allure of dusk.

Throughout the annals of time, Izumo stood as a sanctified realm where the sun bid its nightly farewell. The city's inhabitants gazed upon the descending orange orb with profound reverence, offering prayers that resonated through generations. The tradition of honoring the resplendent sunset over the horizon has endured through ages, a timeless homage to nature's magnificence.

As the golden star gracefully dips below the horizon, casting a radiant glow over the land and the Sea of Japan, it captivates spectators with the ethereal spectacle unfolding before them. This celestial ballet, steeped in ancient legend, stays unaltered since antiquity, painting the sky with hues of divine artistry. The heavens mesmerizingly appear draped in swaths of orange, red and magenta silks.

The gracefully arched coastline, adorned with pristine sands, transitions into a rugged terrain of rocky outcrops to the north, a testament to the divine hand that shaped this land. Witnessing these picturesque vistas, onlookers cannot help but marvel at the craftsmanship that sculpted this landscape into a natural masterpiece.

Across the epochs, the people of Izumo have offered prayers of reverence and honored the setting sun within the sanctified precincts of dedicated shrines. Jutting boldly into the sea, Hinomisaki Cape captures attention with its rugged shores and intricate rock formations, a tapestry woven by the passage of time.

As the sun fades in the celestial expanse,

casting a crimson hue over Inasa no Hama Beach, the silhouette of Bentenjima Island appears against the twilight backdrop. Unfurling southward, the shoreline unveils a captivating panorama, where the scarlet light blends seamlessly with the azure sea—a vision that enchants the soul.

In local folklore, this region of Japan holds a sacred significance as the legendary realm where the gods shaped the fate of the land. The myth recounts a celestial accord among deities culminating in the construction of a palace befitting the divine realm—a hallowed structure revered as the Sunset Shrine, a portal to the realm where the sun bids its farewell.

In the tranquil expanse of the coastline, a poignant duality unfolds as the sun gracefully descends beyond the horizon. Here, amidst the celestial meeting of heavens and earth, an exquisite interplay between peace and tumult takes place. The inhabitants of Izumo, attuned to the essence of their sacred land, watch this cosmic dance, attributing the awe-inspiring grandeur of the sunset to the divine craftsmanship of gods.

Izumo, revered as the realm where the sun submerges beneath the vast sea, embodies a symbolic conduit between realms, weaving a rich tapestry of tranquility and turbulence along its revered shores.

Amid the luminous glow of the sun and the

mystical presence of deities, looms the shadowy figure of the Oni - a malevolent deity shunning the light, dwelling deep within labyrinthine caves and dense forests.

Within the ancient chronicles, teeming with myths and folklore, unfolds a saga of celestial beings and malevolent forces locked in an eternal cosmic ballet. Amidst the shining pantheon of deities and celestial goddesses basking in the sun's gentle caress, lurks the enigmatic beast - a divine ogre enshrouded in darkness and malice. Concealed within the heart of towering mountain sanctuaries, the Oni brandishes a mystical club adorned with amethyst hues, embodying his formidable prowess over thunder and lightning, ensnaring chaos in his wake.

His essence tainted by a haunting predilection for violence and cannibalism, the ogre revels in wanton acts of brutality and destruction. A colossal entity, his formidable countenance boasts formidable horns, lethal fangs, and piercing vermilion eyes. His visage, wild and untamed, features flowing ebony locks and sapphire-hued, banded skin, accentuated by talons adorning his six-fingered hands and feet.

Unleashing pandemonium upon the verdant lands, the resounding thud of the ogre's iron kanabō club reverberates ominously, starting earthquakes and conjuring tsunamis that leave a swath of devastation in their wake. As nature's ire claims lives and spirits fade into the shadows, the Oni prowls the fragile earth, a malign force claiming those entwined in the specter of disaster. A shapeshifter of cunning guile, adept at assuming the guise of a charismatic suitor, the Oni employs deception to ensnare unsuspecting prey, perpetuating his reign of terror with stealth and malevolence.

Passage Two.

Descendant of the Heavens.

Careening from the heavens with a celestial intensity, the pod collided with the snow-dusted peak of Mount Sanbe, hurtling down its slope with a thrilling recklessness. Its wild journey continued along the valley below, until it teetered precariously at the edge of Cape Hino, eventually tumbling down the cliff face and submerging beneath the crashing surf. Despite his restraints, the being within the pod injured his head. He felt a deep, throbbing ache behind his eyes.

In a situation that would evoke panic in most beings, the castaway remained calm, intimately attuned to the surrounding ocean which had shaped his existence back on his home world. The vast seas had been a source of tranquility and communal connection for the Izbek, laying the foundation for his resilience in times of crisis.

Though harboring slim hope of contacting fellow castaways, he clutched his amulet tightly, closed his eyes in telepathic concentration and sent forth prayers. Yet, the silver sphere amid the swaying kelp beds echoed with silence, offering no solace in their return.

Intrigued by his unfamiliar environment, the castaway ventured into the icy waters. He felt the freezing temperatures pierce his frail form like a myriad of needles, a stark contrast to the warm waters of his home world. Battling through the pounding surf, he sought refuge on a nearby beach and dry land, where the intensity of the foreign star above blinded his sensitive eyes and worsened his headache.

Desiring shelter from the harsh light, he sought refuge above the foothills and discovered a cavern. Using the power of his amulet, he transformed the cave into a sanctuary reminiscent of his cherished home on Izbeckia, a place of respite amidst the unfamiliar landscape.

From his secluded vantage point, the extraterrestrial shapeshifter beheld a breathtaking expanse of fertile land, stretching from forested foothills to the boundless sea. The volcanic peak where he had found refuge, though smaller, mirrored the landscapes of his world. Amid this abundant region, tribes of hunter-gatherers thrived, their territories rich with life, fresh water, and the bounty of the seas.

Within this wondrous tapestry of life, majestic creatures roamed freely. Ancient elephants, elk and bison traversed the land, while predatory cats and wolves stalked their prey with primal cunning.

Oni, acknowledging his luck, found that this land provided all he needed for survival - a sanctuary blessed with a mild climate, meandering rivers, verdant forests, and flourishing meadows.

Embracing the guise of the bipedal species for survival, as well as the forms of bison, wolf and tiger, Oni navigated the delicate balance of consumption and adaptation. Each transformation allowed him to derive nutrients from both plant, animal and even humans, asserting his dominance over the land and satiating his glutenous hunger.

To both hunt and survive, Oni chose various creatures as his avatars. Initially, he would transform solely into any of these beasts. But, over time he adapted his transformative powers. Instead of appearing as just one, he transformed into a ghoulish combination of human and the other three animals. In this way the Ogre could eat whatever food source presented itself.

Living in seclusion he awaited rescue in his cave venturing into the woods and valleys to survive when unsuspecting victims crossed his path. Oni survived countless summers and winters never sensing the presence of any of his former shipmates.

In time humans rose with cunning and ruthlessness to claim dominion over the land. Oni, guardian of the underworld, watched as his avatar creatures faded into memory, their calls echoing faintly in the shifting winds of change. No longer could he move unseen, for the once-wild lands yielded to the ordered rows of crops and the lowing of domesticated beasts.

Feeling the encroachment of humanity upon his sacred domain, Oni reached deep into the heart of Mount Sanbe, his amulet pulsing with primal energy. With a thunderous clap of his club against the earth, he summoned forth the elements themselves, twisting smoke, fire, and molten rock from the belly of the slumbering volcano. Purple lightning danced across the sky as he claimed his place of power, burying the majestic cedar trees of Azukihara valley beneath a shroud of lava and ash, a stark reminder of his wrath.

Beneath the hardened crust of the earth, in the hidden petrified forest, Oni forged a sanctuary away from the prying eyes of mortal men. It was a realm of shadows and secrets, where the curious dared not tread, lest they became lost forever in the twisting labyrinth of caves that led to his underground domain.

Yet, even in his hidden refuge, Oni's

solitude was never secure. The shimmering veins of gold that wound through the earth drew the covetous gaze of humans, their greed driving them to invade his home time and time again. Miners spoke in hushed tones of a demonic ogre guarding a forest of riches, a tale that kept most at bay but only served to entice the boldest of souls.

When a samurai of noble lineage dared to venture into the depths, Oni's days of quiet isolation was again under threat. Transforming himself into a guise more befitting the prince of the underworld, he bartered with the warrior, offering gold in exchange for his steed, a calculated move to ward off further incursions.

As the march of civilization brought progress to every corner of the land, Oni found himself increasingly exposed, his powers waning in the face of advancing technology. Guns replaced swords, and fear gave way to ambition, driving humans to seek out the rare earth minerals that lay hidden in his realm.

In a world grown too small for his kind, Oni made a fateful decision to leave Japan, seeking solace in lands untouched by the hands of progress. His journey led him across the vast expanse of the Pacific Ocean, aboard the Lady Washington, the first American vessel to breach the shores of Japan with promises of trade and unknown riches.

Arriving in the untamed wilderness of

Tillamook, along the Oregon coast, Oni felt a spark of recognition stir within him. Intrigued by a primal whisper of danger, Oni heeded the call of his instincts, guiding him away from the encroaching presence of the Europeans. He ventured deep into the heart of the land, seeking refuge from those whose unforgiving gaze threatened to unravel the delicate balance of his existence. With memories of past encounters coloring his beliefs, he knew that these newcomers, with their foreign ways and insatiable thirst for conquest, would be even less forgiving than the Japanese, should they uncover the truth of his nature. And so, shrouded in mystery and cloaked in shadows, Oni moved inland, a silent guardian navigating the realms of both man and spirit, his essence intertwined with the very fabric of the world itself. Amidst towering forests and steaming geysers, he sensed a primal connection to the land, a place where he might find respite from the relentless march of human encroachment.

In the embrace of an ancient volcanic caldera, surrounded by mist-shrouded hills and murmuring rivers, Oni discovered a sanctuary where humans remained dependent on hunting and gathering. In the cool shadows of the dark forests, he found refuge from the harsh light of day, while the earth itself spoke to him in whispers of smoke and vapor, offering him a cavernous home among the untouched wonders of the natural world.

Passage Three.

The Dreaded
Shoshone Ogre.

Deep within the volcanic heart of Yellowstone entrenched in the consciousness of the Tukudika people lives the fearsome Dzoavits. This towering ogre casts a shadow that eclipses the sun and, under the cloak of darkness, abducts and devours children. With a massive horned head adorned with mottled, gnarled black hair resembling a shroud of death, the Dzoavits is a terrifying sight. Its sunken eyes, akin to burning coals, emit a fiendish crimson light, mirroring its insatiable hunger for human flesh. Lured into a cave by cunning animals who pelted it with scorching rocks and sealed the entrance with a massive stone, the Dzoavits unleashes its fury by shaking the land in a relentless attempt to break free.

Passage Four.

A Right of Passage.

The young girl listened to the tribal elders instructing the male warriors before the hunt. Their words steeped in wisdom reverberated in the air. "Without fear, there can be no bravery," they preached amidst the warriors' chanting incantations, evoking the spirits of their ancestors to provide good fortune.

Kimana, whose name conjured images of butterflies dancing in the summertime valleys, harbored boyish passions that defied societal norms. Despite the disapproval from the village elders, Kimana loved the thrill of the hunt. Disinterested in traditional women's roles like weaving, hide sewing, root gathering or cooking, Kimana found her true calling when traversing the hills in pursuit of prey. On this day, the sun ascended into the breathtaking-expansive sky and illuminated Yellowstone in a vibrant tapestry of colors. Kimana slipped out of the Wickiup while her mother and younger siblings slumbered. She untied Satii, her dog and best friend. He would always go with her when she left the village. He was strong and muscular, a direct descendant of the grey wolf and huskies that had migrated south. Together from a distance, they trailed behind the young men.

With such defiance, she had to show herself worthy. At sixteen years old, it was time to prove herself equal to any young brave that underwent this rite of passage into adulthood. Therefore, she knew she could not return to the village without something to show for her hunt. She had, as tradition dictates, painted her face with sacred markings, carrying the weight of generations past upon her sinew-laden limbs. Whispers, murmuring like forgotten lullabies, echoed through her veins. The unsettling thrill of uncertainty gripped her core. The forest leading up the slope was a crucible of life and death. It seemed to breathe with a vitality that both beckoned and repelled.

Though the trees had thinned with autumn's arrival, they still cast a dark foreboding presence. The smell of winter's promise wafted upward from the frost-covered ground. Grizzly Bears had not yet gone to den to hibernate and would be actively seeking food to fatten up before the onset of winter. She would make a nice meal for a ravenous grizzly or the packs of wolves that ran along the ridge above the trees.

Armed with an obsidian knife and a quiver of arrows tipped with the same locally quarried and carved black stone, she felt prepared. She had spent weeks crafting her bow from the horns of a Bighorn sheep, making it pliable by meticulously soaking and shaping it in the hot springs close to her village. It was an exquisite work of craftsmanship and well-constructed. She was a crack shot. Within the untamed forest, beasts both majestic and savage lurked. But it was not only the corporeal beings that sent shivers cascading down her spine. Legends whispered of an evil spirit that haunted caves within these woods, its malevolence rife with a thirst for chaos and despair. The village elders spun campfire stories of children who ventured into the forest never to return, lost forever upon meeting the Dzoavits.

Suddenly, the ground began to shake, heralding the monster's displeasure. To say Kimana was apprehensive would be an understatement. She was terrified. Looking down at Satii, who also looked around furtively, she searched for woodpecker feathers so she could perform the jumping dance to ward off the monster and his shaking of the ground. Kimana truly hoped the sheep tracks that Satii had sniffed out would lead her to her prey and allow her to make a clean kill and return home. They had followed the prints across the stream, where they turned up the slope to an area beyond the trees. Strangely, another set of tracks had joined the trail, unusual in their appearance. It was the tracks of a four-legged creature with a peculiar half-moon footprint. The telltale sign of a horse, most probably that of a Crow tribal warrior. Pondering what would happen if she happened upon a rival hunting party, she considered abandoning the hunt and seeking out a fresh set of tracks to follow. The Crow, unlike her own tribe, embraced hunting on horseback and were formidable in battle. Satii, after sniffing once more at the ground, looked up at her. Its face betrayed the dog's concern. Without a sound, Satii's deep brown eyes pleaded with Kimana to be quiet and careful as they stealthily climbed the hill.

However, she was suddenly frozen in place by the otherworldly sound of an animal or man in pain. While catching her breath, a massive form charged her at full speed. Its snorting nostrils and wide eyes betrayed its intent to escape. The horse swerved, scattering shreds of beaded buffalo hide, knocking her to the ground with tremendous force. As it rushed past Satii, she saw terror in its eyes, deep gashes along its flanks and a trailing blanket and saddle decorated with beads and tribal markings.

Once again, as she tried to rise to her feet, the ground began to shake. She heard the piercing cry once more of a wounded creature. A bone-chilling roar followed, one suffused with savagery but also with satisfaction. Drawing her bow, she nocked an arrow and crept cautiously up the hill. Upon reaching the lip, she paused, taking in the sight that filled her with terror.

On the ground lay a Crow horse soldier, still alive but barely. Standing over him and devouring his flesh was the Dzoavits who had escaped its cavernous prison. Suddenly, the monster reared up, its ugly, black-hairy form now standing eight feet tall, with remnants of flesh, saliva, and blood cascading from its mouth. It turned its head towards them and growled. Satii was now barking and snarling uncontrollably. The young hunter released her arrow and retrieved a piece of the blood-soaked beaded buffalo hide. She turned to flee. Grabbing Satii, who she feared might confront this monster, she pointed him down the hill and encouraged him to run. Tumbling down the slope at breakneck speed, her trembling limbs stumbled across the stream, her breath ragged and frantic. The haunting echoes of the Dzoavits' menacing roar followed in her wake, driving her feet to move ever faster. Satii kept cadence to be constantly by her side.

Her heart raced, a drumbeat of sheer adrenaline pulsating through her veins, urging her forward. Leaping over fallen branches and gnarled roots with the same agility as her loyal dog, she longed to return to the safety of the village. She briefly wished she were helping her mother with household chores. Through the trees that began to thin, she glimpsed the smoking valley floor, the winding river and the geysers looking like shimmering crystals as they bathed in the golden glow of sunshine. With a final burst of determination, Kimana and Satii exploded out of the trees towards sanctuary.

Stumbling upon the open clearing, her legs finally gave way beneath her. Her trembling arms pulled Satii towards her, with her fingers clutching his soft fur. She grounded herself in the tangible reality of safety. Her chest heaved with grateful gasps of air as she gazed up at the sky, listened to the soothing sound of the rippling river and breathed in the sweet smell of freedom that drifted on the autumn wind. The ground, for now, had stopped trembling and they had left that terrible scene of carnage far behind in the distance. She stared down at the blood-soaked beadwork, her only trophy to prove her bravery and she contemplated the Crow warrior's unthinkable fate.

To this day, when the underworld rumbles and the wind rustles the trees, the ghostly voices of the Oni's victims forever haunt Yellowstone.

STORY TWO.

THE WHITE BEAR GODDESS

Passage One.

The Legend.

A raging winter storm howled outside, snowflakes pirouetting in the frigid air as a divine presence descended from the heavens. Nanuk, the Polar Bear Shapeshifter Goddess, appeared in a breathtaking spectacle, encased in a colossal silver snowball that landed gracefully on the icy tundra. Nanuk embodied winter's essence and the hunt, her purpose intricately woven into nature's rhythm. With each stride upon the icy ground, the earth quivered in homage and Arctic creatures knelt in reverence. Gentle and compassionate, she safeguarded life's delicate equilibrium, yet her ferocity and power were renowned—a force capable of toppling mountains with a mere swipe of her paw. In her human guise, Nanuk was captivating. Her snowy white skin exuded an otherworldly radiance, setting off the darkness of her jet-black hair that flowed like a waterfall. Her deep ebony eyes reflected the profound depth of the Arctic night sky, shimmering with ancient wisdom. Always at her side was a magnificent crystal, imbued with winter's enchantment. Nanuk used this artifact to conjure snowflakes and icy winds, spreading winter's embrace across her world. She crafted an exquisite ice palace amid the frozen mountains— a magnificent abode from which she ruled with unparalleled grace. Nanuk embodied the balance of beauty and power, nurturing and fierce. Her presence commanded respect, instilling awe, and reverence. In her wintry realm, she reigned as a majestic guardian, ensuring harmony and survival for all her creatures.

Passage Two.

The Clash of Cultures.

In Greenland's rugged lands, two great civilizations clashed. The Vikings, led by Thorfinn Karlsefni, arrived to colonize the territory, their longboats slicing through frigid waters. Opposing them were the Inuit, Greenland's native inhabitants, watching the newcomers with curiosity and caution, their sharp eyes reflecting the piercing winds. Greenland's raw beauty captivated Thorfinn and his men with its jagged cliffs and fjords, presenting a striking backdrop to their ambitions. Clad in furs and armed with swords as sharp as northern stars, the Vikings felt whirlwinds of excitement coursing through their veins. In contrast, the Inuit moved with grace across the frozen landscape, their sleek kayaks gliding over icy waters. They shared a deep connection to the land, each footstep echoing ancestral wisdom. Though their weapons appeared crude compared to the Vikings' arsenal, the Inuit honed each harpoon and knife to deadly precision. As the Vikings set up settlements, unfurling their red-and-white banners, the Inuit watched with awe and apprehension. While understanding the Norsemen's thirst for exploration, a protectiveness stirred within the Inuit. This was their home. Communication became a challenge, a dance of gestures and fleeting expressions. The Norsemen tried to swap trinkets for the Inuit's treasures, laughter traded for curiosity. Despite divergent languages, a fragile understanding took shape. A delicate ice bridge spanning a frozen fjord. Yet fate had other plans. A Norse bull, startled by its unfamiliar surroundings, broke free and galloped through the Inuit village. Chaos ensued as they interpreted the bull's flight as aggression, sparking fear and confusion that spread like embers on a frosty night, fueling conflict. With anguished cries and a clash of steel, the Inuit launched an attack. The air vibrated with the clash of worlds and the cries of men. Unity in curiosity transformed into a dance of survival, weapons gleaming like ice shards in the pale sunlight. The Vikings, their swords unsheathed and shields clashing with fury, stood unwavering. However, the Inuit fought with primal grace, their harpoons finding their mark with precision.

Guided by ancestral whispers, their bond with the land was profound. Amidst the chaos, a figure suddenly appeared from a tornado of ice and snow. Enveloped by a swirling blizzard and the crackling of purple lightning bolts, Nanuk, the polar bear goddess appeared. Her glistening white fur stark against the snow-laden landscape, as she advanced with an aura of power. Her ice-blue eyes held wisdom beyond mortal struggles. Silence enveloped the land as all attention turned to Nanuk. Towering over them, her thick white fur glistened like moonlit snow, while her crystalline eyes exuded wisdom and power. Nanuk's voice echoed through the frozen valleys, compelling both the Vikings and the Inuit to lower their weapons and embrace peace. Entranced by her presence, a sense of awe and unity washed over them, transcending cultural boundaries.

Nanuk spoke of the land's potential for harmony and collaboration, weaving tales of bountiful rivers and unexplored horizons. She conjured visions of the Northern Lights and ancient spirits, guiding them toward mutual comprehension and cooperation.

In a pivotal moment, the Vikings and Inuit exchanged knowing glances, acknowledging their intertwined fates. Thorfinn extended a hand of friendship, met with resolute acceptance by the Inuit leaders, marking the dawn of a new alliance founded on mutual regard and collaboration.

United by a common purpose, the Vikings and Inuit embarked on a journey toward concord, blending their knowledge and skills. Through shared teachings and joint endeavors, they gleaned wisdom from each other, nurturing a bond that transcended past strife. As seasons unfolded under Nanuk's vigilant gaze, Greenland blossomed into a testament to unity's might. The once-antagonistic civilizations prospered in harmony, crafting a legacy of resilience, empathy, and cooperation. The people of Greenland reflected on their shared past with gratitude, venerating Nanuk as the catalyst for their unity. A monumental totem depicting Nanuk clutching a magical amulet symbolized their collective odyssey and enduring accord, a reminder of peace triumphing over discord.

With their ancestors' spirits as witnesses, the Vikings and Inuit embraced the everlasting ties forged amidst the clash of civilizations, bequeathing a legacy of unity and coexistence in

Greenland's rugged terrains.

Passage Three.

The Goddess's Legacy.

In the remote village of Inuktitut, nestled on the Arctic's icy shores, lived a young Inuit hunter named Malak. With his harpoon in hand, he ventured onto the frozen polar ice sheet, guided by the light of the full moon and the ancient stories shared by his wise grandfather, who constantly assured him of his special destiny.

"You possess a power within you that is extraordinary," his grandfather would say, comforting Malak whenever he felt unsure.

On this day, as Malak crept closer to his prey, his grandfather's words echoed in his head. The ice beneath his feet creaked and groaned, but he ignored the unsettling sounds, knowing the importance of patience and focus. Fate however had a different plan in store for him. With an earth-shattering crack, the ice split open beneath him, plunging him into the freezing depths of the Arctic Sea.

As his body sank, Malak's consciousness began to fade. The icy coldness embraced him, draining his strength. Just as he was about to succumb to the dark depths, a vision appeared before his eyes. A colossal white polar bear, its fur shimmering like freshly fallen snow, swam gracefully towards him, guiding him to the surface with its immense strength. The bear's eyes gleamed with a curious wisdom beyond ordinary animals.

Malak awoke on the sandy beach, shivering and weak. As he gathered his thoughts, the warm whispers of his grandfather's stories floated through his mind. According to ancient legends, those chosen to carry the spirit of the polar bear had incredible strength, wisdom, and a deep connection to Nanuk herself.

Returning to the village, Malak sought his grandfather's counsel. "Grandfather!" he shouted breathlessly. Once he gathered his thoughts, he recounted his harrowing experience.

With a twinkle in his eyes, the elder confirmed what Malak had suspected. Nanuk had chosen his grandson to carry her spirit within him. Skeptical at first, all doubt vanished when during the next full moon, he transformed into a majestic snow-colored bear.

Embracing his newfound destiny, Malak trained meticulously under his grandfather's tutelage. He felt a harmonious bond with nature, guided by the teachings of his ancestors and the indomitable spirit of the polar bear.

As time passed, Malak faced a myriad of challenges and adversaries, but Nanuk's spirit guided him to protect his village. In this frozen landscape and close-knit community, Malak's legend grew. His story—of courage, resilience and the bond between man and nature—served as a reminder to all young people worldwide to listen to the wilderness, for within those whispers lay the secrets of their true potential.

Passage Four.

Magic Totems of the Gods.

Embark from Nuuk, Greenland's largest city, up the Nuup Kangerlau fjord into the remote backcountry and you will discover the captivating Inuit settlement of Kapisillit. Here, amidst cobalt blue waters, the majestic Sermitsiaq mountain towers above, its sharp ridges cutting through ribbons of ice and snow. Immense glaciers pour water into the fjord from the retreating Greenland Ice Sheet, while scattered skerries guide the way to the Labrador Sea.

In this mesmerizing setting lives Aron Enoksen, an Inuit craftsman and artisan. His modest hut and workshop, nestled in a quiet snow-covered alley, serve as a sanctuary where he refines his craft. Through frost-covered windows, a meager fluorescent light brightens the dimly lit room. A narrow gap in the doorway ushers in the frigid Arctic air, casting a solitary beam that illuminates countless specks of dust swirling like delicate snowflakes. Inside, a lone iron stove struggles to spread warmth.

Aron stands as one of the few remaining traditional artists practicing the ancient art of carving Tupilaks or totems. These sacred figures, revered for their power and magic, hold immense significance in Inuit culture.

In the Arctic chill, Aron employs age-old techniques handed down through generations. His fingers, toughened by the cold, skillfully carve intricate details into bone, wood, and soapstone. Every stroke of his tools infuses life into his creations, as if guided by the ancestors themselves.

Aron's workshop is a treasury of sacred materials. Bundles of narwhal tusks, driftwood, and sealskin rest on wooden shelves alongside traditional Inuit knives and chisels. The rhythmic sound of carving mingles with the faint crackling of the stove.

In the dim light, the finished Tupilaks stand proudly, their carved eyes gleaming with ancient wisdom. Depicting fantastical creatures merging human and animal traits, they evoke a sense of reverence and wonder. Each figure carries a unique tale, a link to the spirits of the past, ensuring their legacy endures.

Recognizing the importance of his role as a guardian of tradition, Aron imparts his knowledge and skills to aspiring artisans in the village. Together, they uphold the ancient art of totem carving, ensuring that the ancestral spirits continue to safeguard and inspire future generations.

The villagers of Kapisillit hold Aron and his craft in high esteem. His workshop, though unassuming, stands as a symbol of resilience, culture and the enduring bond between the Inuit people and their heritage. So long as his hands continue to carve, the spirits of the ancestors will forever dwell within the sacred totems, guiding and protecting the community.

Aron now spends most days meticulously crafting Tupilaks inspired by polar bears from walrus tusks and bone. Through his skilled hands, the essence of these majestic creatures transforms into everyday objects like rings, pendants, and bracelets. These pieces find their way to traders in Nuuk, catering to the increasing number of tourists seeking a memento of their journey—a talisman believed to tap into the protective energies of their ancestors.

Occasionally, drawing upon his unique gift, Aron breathes life into a whale tooth, a rib bone or even an entire walrus skull adorned with magnificent tusks. From these materials, he conjures hidden figures that take shape in his creative mind. Using only traditional tools, he creates exquisite artworks, capturing the playful essence of age-old traditions—a tribute to the rich cultural heritage passed down through the ages. Aron produces no more than ten of these exceptional pieces annually, eagerly sought after by collectors yearning to behold totemic representations of joyous and fearsome faces, mysterious creatures, and whimsical portrayals of sea animals. His true masterpieces proclaiming the presence of Nanuk, the polar bear goddess, remain exclusively reserved for dealers who buy his work for affluent patrons in Canada, Denmark, and the USA.

Behind his workbench was a collection of ceremonial headdresses, clothing, and weapons. Perched upon a shelf above them sat a small figurine of Nanuk, the shape-shifting polar bear. Generations of Inuit shamans had passed down this treasured objet d'art. Nanuk, with her sleek alabaster form, deep ebony eyes and toned muscles, held a mystical allure. Her origin remained shrouded in mystery. Many believed an ancient hunter fashioned her when he came across the goddess and instead of attacking her, laid down his harpoon. In respect, Nanuk donated to him a rib bone from which he fashioned an homage to her beauty and power.

The Inuit revered this Tupilak of Nanuk as the embodiment of the bear goddess. They believed it had powers not only to guard against malevolent spirits and diseases, but also, if wielded by a descendant of the goddess, to create lightning and summon almighty tempests. Nanuk, from her vantage point protected Aron and the community. Despite being offered significant amounts of money, especially by one persistent Scandinavian collector, Aron remained resolute. This Tupilak belonged to the Inuit tribe and was not for sale.

Passage Five.

The Plight of the Arctic Bear.

Descending from an ancient lineage of Inuit hunters and Viking warriors, Malak Malaksen carried the spirit of Nanuk inside him. Recently, he had chosen to ship a crate brimming with Aron's intricate sculptures depicting polar bears to Northern England instead of his London office branch at the Wildlife Foundation. As part of a global initiative to reverse the declining populations of these majestic white bears, Malak's mission was to awaken the increasingly apathetic societies to their plight. In his efforts to raise funds and amplify outreach, Malak intended to make these revered Inuit totems available for sale during the upcoming symposium at the Yorkshire Wildlife Park. The park, priding itself as the sole Arctic Ambassador Center for Polar Bears International in the United Kingdom, would serve as a platform to engage in open conversations about the art and the precarious predicament of these creatures. Ever since leaving Greenland and his grandfather's teachings, Malak's singular goal had been to find a way to save the very beings he could transform into. To everyone who would listen, he preached his profound belief that "We simply have to preserve these beautiful creatures and their habitat."

He stayed steadfast in his commitment to educate humanity about the peril all arctic animals faced.

In just decades, a staggering eighty-four thousand square miles of sea ice, vital for the bears' survival, had vanished, leading to the imminent collapse of their populations. While polar bears are known to thrive in some of the planet's harshest conditions, it is the exact opposite that poses a threat. The escalated global temperatures have caused their icy habitat to gradually fade away, pushing them perilously close to extinction. Malak was painfully aware that the crucial solution lay in preserving the sea ice, a feat that would need a significant reduction in fossil fuel consumption.

Boarding the train at King's Cross Station, unaware of the extent of his impact, Malak embarked on a journey that was destined to profoundly influence his kindred animals. As the train rhythmically traversed the English countryside, Malak's thoughts drifted to the arctic expanse of Greenland and the ethereal beauty of Nanuk, the polar bear goddess who had chosen him to bear her spirit. The weight of his mission to raise awareness and support for the imperiled polar bears lay heavy on his heart. It drove him forward with a fervent determination.

A flurry of activity and anticipation greeted Malak as he arrived at the Wildlife Park. The symposium was a gathering of conservationists, researchers, and nature enthusiasts from across the globe, all united in their shared concern for the plight of the polar bears and the rapidly changing Arctic environment.

Setting up his exhibit of Aron's exquisite totems, each intricately carved with reverence and skill, Malak felt a surge of pride and purpose. Clutching a polar bear pendant gifted by his grandfather, he knew that these creations were not just works of art; they were vessels of heritage and tradition, symbols of the sacred connection between humanity and the natural world.

As visitors streamed in, drawn by the allure of the totems and the urgency of the cause they stood for, Malak engaged them in conversations about the significance of preserving the Arctic ecosystem and its iconic inhabitants. He spoke of Nanuk, the guardian spirit of the polar bears and the need to honor her legacy by protecting her earthly kin. One visitor who introduced himself as Karl Thorfinnssen seemed enthusiastic not only by the tupilaks but by Malak himself. It seemed a little disconcerting, but Malak shrugged off the disquieting feeling and concentrated on his mission.

Throughout the symposium, Malak shared his personal story of transformation and awakening to the interconnectedness of all life. His words resonated with many, sparking a collective sense of responsibility and empowerment. People from diverse backgrounds and cultures came together, inspired by Malak's passion and commitment to making a difference.

As the event ended, the totems crafted by Aron became beacons of hope and unity. Each purchase made contributed to the vital conservation efforts aimed at safeguarding the future of the polar bears and their fragile ecosystem. Malak's message and people's newfound awareness and solidarity signaled an influx of support and donations.

As Malak bid farewell to the Yorkshire Wildlife Park, a sense of fulfillment and determination coursed through his veins. The interactions, the connections made, and the impact created fueled his resolve to continue his mission with even greater fervor. Little did he know that he had a malevolent chaperone, lurking in the shadows that had been trailing his every move since he left Greenland.

Karl Thorfinnssen was a direct descendant of the Viking warrior that had recounted the tale of Nanuk in his Saga and Karl was determined to gain that ancestral power for himself. Malak he was sure could unlock the power of the mysterious Inuit totem sitting in Aron Enoksens workshop.

Passage Six.

Power Protected.

Unbeknownst to Malak, a web of intrigue and conspiracy had woven its threads around the polar bear totems he had displayed. The totems, imbued with ancestral spirits and crafted with traditional knowledge, held a power that extended beyond mere artistry. Rumors whispered among the darkened alleys of the art world spoke of a hidden energy within Aron's creations—a force that could potentially shift the balance of power in the natural order.

As Malak boarded the flight back to Greenland from London Heathrow Airport, the figure of Karl Thorfinnssen, cloaked in shadows, watched from a distance, eyes gleaming with a malevolent glint.

Meanwhile, back in Greenland, Aron Enoksen labored tirelessly in his workshop, unaware of the peril that loomed on the horizon. The meticulously crafted totem above his workbench held a secret that few knew. It carried a connection to Nanuk, the polar bear goddess. It wielded power for both good and ill.

As the hours stretched into the night, a chilling wind whispered through the cracks of his hut, carrying with it an ominous foreboding of impending danger.

In London, a meeting took place in the dimly lit chambers of a clandestine group controlled by Thorfinnssen, The Collector. They were known only as Sons of the Norseman. Comprising shadowy figures with an agenda to restore Viking supremacy, this group plotted in hushed tones shrouded in secrecy. The Collector sat at the head of the table, his eyes fixed on a map of Greenland and the location of Aron's secluded workshop.

The stage was set for a showdown of epic proportions—a clash between the forces of light and darkness, conservation, and exploitation. Malak and Aron, with the totem for protection fell into a perilous game of cat and mouse, where the stakes were higher than they could have ever imagined.

As Malak landed in Nuuk, a shroud-like sense of unease settled over him. The whispers of the Arctic winds carried a warning, a primal instinct urging him to be vigilant. Little did he know that danger was drawing closer with each passing moment. He was heading towards a confrontation that would test his courage, resolve and the very essence of his bond with Nanuk.

In the darkness of the Arctic night, figures prowled the frozen landscape, hooded, and cloaked, their steps silent as a specters. Karl

Thorfinnssen, driven by his insatiable lust for power, had set his sights on the polar bear totem, intent on claiming its ancient energy for his own nefarious purposes.

Aron, sensing a disturbance in the natural balance, grabbed his tools with a steely determination. The ancestral spirits within his creation stirred, whispering warnings of impending danger. The time had come for him to protect not just his art but the sacred connection it held with the spirit of Nanuk.

Malak felt like an unknown voice was calling him. Whispers of attraction rebounded in his head, beckoning him towards Aron's workshop. The air grew dense with tension, his instincts on high alert. The winds were now blowing the falling snow in white sheets across the park, carrying a faint scent of treachery, a premonition of the impending clash that would pit him against forces darker and more insidious than he had ever faced before.

As Malak moved towards the building, a sudden shift in the air brought a chill down his spine. The familiar presence of Nanuk, the Polar Bear Shapeshifter Goddess, washed over him, urging him to be alert. The storm was beginning to clear, but a new danger loomed in the shadows.

A dark figure appeared from the swirling snow, cloaked in mystery and malice. The Collector craved to harness Malak and Nanuk's power for his twisted ambitions. "Hello Malak," Karl sneered, his eyes gleaming with a cruel light. Malak's hand tightened around his pendant that held Nanuk's essence, ready for the confrontation ahead. "What Do You Want?" Malak's voice was firm, laced with an underlying threat.

The Collector chuckled darkly, a chilling sound that echoed in the stillness of the night. "Oh Malak, you underestimate the gift within you. You do not deserve to wield such power. I on the other hand am destined to do so. I will claim Nanuk's spirit for myself and your abilities will help me unlock them."

With a flick of his wrist, Thorfinnssen produced what looked like an aerosol spray can and unleashed a malevolent green haze towards Malak, trying to stun him as other armed assailants with nets now joined the fray.

Quick as lightning, Malak dodged the attack and summoned the spirit of Nanuk to aid him. The air crackled with energy as the goddess manifested in all her majestic glory. "You will not succeed. The power of the White Bear is not yours to command."

Nanuk's voice was so loud it caused the snow to topple from the workshop roof. A fierce battle ensued. As Karl Thorfinnssen and his cohorts tried to encircle the bear and entangle it in their nets, Nanuk roared and clawed her displeasure. Nanuk's strength proved to be formidable. With a final surge of power, Malak, calling on the sacred totem, unleashed a blinding light that engulfed Karl and his cohorts, leveling them to the ground and vanquishing the darkness that clouded their hearts. As the dust settled, Malak, as the majestic bear, stood victorious. However, the threat of others seeking the Inuit goddess's power lingered in the air.

As he turned towards Aron's workshop, Malak saw Aron standing at the door, a mixture of relief and concern on his face.

"We have stopped this attempt, but the true danger lies in the shadows. We must be vigilant, for darkness has many faces."

And with those words, Nanuk once more left his body and vanished into the ether, leaving Malak to ponder the mysteries that unfolded before him. The road ahead was fraught with peril and uncertainty, but Malak knew one thing for certain – the White Bear Goddess would always stand with him, guiding him towards a destiny that held the fate of both worlds in its balance.

The snow had stopped falling and the wind had abated. Malak stood in the silence of the Arctic night, the glow of the moon casting a silvery light over the landscape. The echoes of Nanuk's voice still resonated within him, a powerful reminder of the responsibility he bore. The shadows that Karl and his followers left behind would not be the last threat. Malak knew he had to be vigilant and resilient, for the battle to protect the polar bears and their habitat was just beginning.

"Aron, we need to prepare," Malak said, his voice steady. "Karl's defeat will not stop others from seeking the power of Nanuk. We must safeguard these sacred totems and continue our mission to protect the Arctic and its inhabitants."

As Malak stood beneath the twinkling starlit sky, a surge of determination coursed through his veins, igniting a fire within him. With a fierce resolve burning in his eyes, he felt a deep sense of purpose pulsating through every fiber of his being. The challenges ahead loomed large, casting daunting shadows, but he stood undaunted, fortified by the guidance of Nanuk and the unwavering support of his allies who shared his fervor for the cause.

The journey to safeguard the majestic polar bears and their vanishing habitat was a treacherous one, fraught with perils and uncertainties. Yet, Malak was resolute in his commitment to see it through to the very end. The fate of these magnificent creatures rested heavily on his shoulders, a weight he bore with unwavering determination and boundless courage.

In the heart of the unforgiving Arctic expanse, amidst the pristine snow and shimmering ice, a new chapter was unfolding—a saga of hope, resilience, and unyielding dedication

to the preservation of the natural world.

STORY THREE.

THE RAINBOW DRAGON.

Passage One.

A Paradoxical Beauty.

In a realm where celestial beauty intertwines with immense power, a being of awe-inspiring grace descends from the heavens above. The Culebre, a hermaphroditic dragon god, appears from a fiery egg—a vessel of divine creation hurled from the stars onto the surface of the earth. Its presence reminds mortals of the omnipotent force that birthed the very essence of creation.

As the Culebre unfurls its wings, a shimmering cascade of colors captivates all who dare to look. Hypnotic amber eyes, brimming with intelligence and compassion, peer into the souls of those who revere the deity's magnificence. Within the depths of the mountain caves of Asturia, the Culebre carves its dwelling, a sanctuary of solitude and tranquility.

Sharp claws and webbed wings accentuate the dragon god's mighty form, while a resplendent head adorned with vibrant feathers highlights its otherworldly aesthetic. This paradoxical beauty emanates from its soul, transcending its non-binary nature and traditional gender boundaries. The Culebre is a testament to the exquisite balance found within the harmonious embrace of both masculine and feminine energies.

Wherever it roams, the Culebre becomes elusive, enshrouding itself in smoke clouds and mist that billow gracefully in its wake. It is a shapeshifter of extraordinary prowess, seamlessly transforming into a breathtaking vision, neither man nor woman but both handsome and strikingly beautiful. This versatility embodies the fluidity of its divine essence, a celestial being unrestricted by a singular form.

Gently cradled within its palm, the Culebre carries a jewel of transcendent power, a purple cintamani radiating mystical energy. It is a reminder of the deity's extraordinary abilities, a conduit through which the extraordinary becomes possible.

Among its kind, the Culebre was the ninth to descend from the skies, a number of profound significance. Adorning its back are nine majestic ridges, each representing a fragment of its divine lineage. Eighty-one scales glimmer with ancient wisdom, reminding everyone of the sacred nature of its existence.

September holds sway over the Culebre's divine realm, the ninth month and one of transition and abundant life. As the protector of crops and the benefactor of agriculture, the dragon god harnesses its power to summon rain clouds during times of drought. With a voice that resonates through valleys, it calls upon the sun to caress the fields, ripening them to a bountiful harvest. Guiding humanity towards sustenance and prosperity, the Culebre's benevolence echoes in grain stalks swaying in the wind and every fruit tree reaching for the sky.

In the very core of this being of dualistic beauty lies a wellspring of wonder, power, and compassion. The Culebre, revered and respected as a guardian, symbolizes the intricate tapestry that weaves together the celestial and earthly realms.

Passage Two.

A New Journey.

Scheduled as the ninth pod to be jettisoned from the mothership, they followed behind their life partner, with whom they shared a profound emotional connection. An undeniable trepidation emanated from their amber eyes.

Since their earliest days on Izbeckia, the number nine had held deep significance—a symbol of luck and importance. Appearing from the vast sea after nine cycles of lunar interchanges, they had earned a similar number of meritorious citations during their coming-of-age ceremony. Taking a deep breath, echoing the pod's departure, doubts lingered, questioning the decision to stay on this perilous planet. Yet, after consulting their soulmate, who reassured them they would face the unknown together, they found comfort in their shapeshifting prowess—a unique ability that would prove invaluable for their survival.

The pod settled on a slope, offering a mesmerizing view of a fertile valley and a meandering river flowing towards the vast sea. Towering mountains of granite, dusted with a pristine layer of ethereal white, formed an impenetrable barrier behind them. The valley below captivated them, teeming with creatures they had never seen before. Grazing by the babbling waters and quenching their thirst from the river, these unknown beings sparked an insatiable curiosity. Clutching their amulet tightly, they realized that neither their beloved partner nor any other Izbek were nearby, signaling they would have to face the trials of survival alone. A wave of sadness and uncertainty washed over them, wondering if they would ever be rescued.

With cautious intrigue, they kept a safe distance, silently watching the intricate tapestry of life unfolding in this new world. Among the inhabitants, two distinct bipedal species competed for the abundant resources within the valley. Seeking shelter, they made their home in an expansive cave. Using the power of their amulet, they transformed the cavern into a comfortable sanctuary reminiscent of their home on Izbeckia. Within its depths, astonishing revelations awaited them—ancient paintings adorning the walls depicted animals, hunts and a spectacular panorama of the night sky created by primitive primates.

Amidst these captivating artworks, a particular celestial beast caught their attention. Depicted as a winged creature conjured from blazing bonfires, they were unaware that this image originated from the imagination of ancient humans, recounting tales of immense creatures whose bones they found unearthed along the riverbank. They experienced visions, influenced by fermented and decaying fruits, with tendrils of smoke weaving fantastical tales into their minds.

Driven by insatiable curiosity, the Izbek survivor assumed the forms of both the mythical creature on the cave wall and one of the two hominid species inhabiting the valley. Little did they realize that these Neanderthals would eventually succumb to the rising dominance of Homo sapiens and fade into the annals of history. Understanding the need to form alliances with the dominant species for survival, they briefly took to the skies, gracefully navigating the land when liberated from prying eyes. Feasting upon untamed herds of wild cattle grazing in the fertile valley and indulging in bountiful tuna schools swimming wildly in the Bay of Biscay, they nourished themselves while keeping a majestic disguise.

Nurturing and guiding the early hunter-gatherers, they bestowed upon them the knowledge of cultivation and animal husbandry, embracing a life of abundance and ease. Within the pristine valley and majestic mountains lay fertile grasslands, blessed with abundant water and untapped treasures waiting to be discovered. Unveiling the secrets of extracting coal and zinc, they enlightened their people on the intricacies of mining, smelting and metallurgy. As a magnificent dragon, they stood as a protector of their cherished community, revered, and worshipped as a deity by their devoted followers.

Nestled within the protective embrace of

the mountains, the Celtic civilization thrived in what is now modern-day Spain. This community flourished under the watchful care of the Culebre. Yet, as time passed, the Culebre patiently awaited rescue in the sanctuary of their cave. Sometimes, they felt the presence of other Izbek, also yearning for rescue and hoping it was their beloved; yet none dared to venture into their realm. Centuries passed and with new enlightenment, humans abandoned pagan beliefs and mythical creatures. Seduced by the allure of Christianity, their people turned away from the dragon, leaving them feeling isolated and seeking comfort in their human guise. Yet, despite their captivating nature, their non-binary existence prevented true acceptance.

As Spain succumbed to the Moors' dominance, the lands of Asturias faced imminent peril. In the profound battle of Covadonga, the Asturians repelled the Islamic forces and claimed their independence. Though the Culebre played a vital role, using their mythical amulet to aid their victory, the people credited the symbolic intercession and triumph to the benevolence of a divine statue of the Virgin Mary known as 'Our Lady of Covadonga.'

Recognizing the shifting beliefs of their people, the Culebre chose to leave the land they had called home for millennia, embarking on a journey to reunite with their fellow castaway loved one and seek news of impending rescue.

However, as days turned into weeks, weeks into years and years into centuries, they became a nomadic wanderer. Hindered by their homogeneous appearance, assimilation into any community proved a constant struggle, leaving the Culebre in perpetual motion.

Transforming into their majestic dragon self often led to fear, compelling them to continue their travels. Perceived as an evil spirit and a harbinger of destruction in the Middle East and viewed as an untrustworthy trickster in Asia Minor and India, their journey pressed on.

Like a nomadic wisp drifting through the sky, the Culebre dragon traversed the vast expanse of continents, finally finding a home in ancient China.

Nestled amongst the breathtaking beauty of the Qilian rainbow mountains, the Culebre settled into a sanctuary that mirrored its very soul. The rocks of Zhangye Danxia, adorned with a vibrant palette of maroon, magenta and lemon hues, towered overhead, reaching countless feet into the heavens. Each crevice and curve spoke a silent language, paying homage to the rich history of the land. With a head bearing magnificent feathers blending into the kaleidoscope of colors, the Culebre made a home within the labyrinthine canyons of this enchanting landscape. As the dragon soared through the skies, the people below gazed skyward in awe, their eyes filled with reverence. To them, this resplendent creature embodied the harmonious unity of Yin and Yang, a captivating symbol of duality.

Known for its folklore and legends, China welcomed the dragon shapeshifter with open arms. The people believed that the Culebre was divine, sent to bring prosperity and protection to their land. Embracing the customs and traditions of this enchanting country, the Culebre reveled in the rich tapestry of Chinese culture. Becoming a mentor and advisor to the villagers, guiding them through hardships and celebrating their triumphs, the dragon shapeshifter used its ability to shift between genders to connect with the people on a deeper level, transcending the binary societal norms that often stifled its true essence. Utilizing its magical amulet, the Culebre created an extraordinary era of peace and prosperity.

Yet, amidst this newfound acceptance, powerful memories stirred within the Culebre's soul. It could not help but wonder about its soulmate and fellow Izbek castaways who had journeyed alongside in times long past. With its mystical purple amulet clasped tightly in its talons, the dragon sensed a haunting absence, a land devoid of its kind. The Izbek had left long ago, but the echoes of their presence reverberated through the land.

A marvelous sight revealed itself as the

Culebre beheld the grandeur of the Pyramid-shaped Necropolis, an earthly marvel crafted from pressed soil and colossal stones. Behind its unassuming facade lay an empire of terracotta warriors, chariots, and majestic equine companions, all poised to go with Emperor Qin Shi Huang to the realm beyond. Ethereal rivers of liquid mercury wove their way amidst this magnificent army, casting a shimmering glow upon the walls. Constellations painted the ceiling, celestial bodies not even visible from Earth, a testament to the knowledge imparted by the Izbek. Monoliths punctuated the landscape, adorned with intricate astronomical calculations, a testament to the depths of wisdom bestowed upon the people by the Culebre's kin.

A question tugged at the dragon's heart: why had the Izbek departed this sacred land? Was it an act of choice or born of unspeakable tragedy? Had their companion at one time graced this land? Could one of their cherished crew mates now rest eternally within the triangular walls of the elaborate tomb? The Culebre's wings sliced through the air, carrying them across the expanse of this enigmatic land. As they soared amidst the echoes of their fellow travelers, the dragon pondered the mystery that had led them here, their presence an eternal enigma etched upon this beguiling corner of the planet.

Passage Three.

A Path to Riches.

Nestled high on the Loess Plateau in the heart of China lay the ancient city of Qingjian. Here, Yaodong dwellings carved into the steep hillsides offered relief from the summer heat, while in the winter months, they radiated warmth from the clay walls. These dwellings, resembling arched structures rising from the earth, formed a majestic network of wooden ladders and stone floors, clustering together like the burrows of nesting sand martins along a riverbank.

Within this community, a young girl named Peiling Zhao blossomed. Born on the ninth day of the ninth month in the Year of the Dragon, she had an entwined connection with that mystical creature to which she prayed periodically for guidance. With her tomboyish spirit, she tended to and rode horses, outshining the boys in her village and the surrounding countryside.

As the Lunar New Year approached, a chance for change dangled before her in the form of a journey to Chang'an City. Traders recognized Peiling's formidable talent on horseback and offered her family a fortune to apprentice her as a polo rider in the grand city. Reluctant at first, her father eventually agreed, knowing this opportunity could lift his family out of poverty.

Although hesitant to leave the only home she had ever known, Peiling's excitement bubbled within her. The prospect of leaving the clay dirt behind and setting off on an adventure filled her heart with anticipation. Accompanied by her eldest brother, they embarked on their journey towards Chang'an, a city perched gracefully north of the Wei River. Its majestic walls, moat and canals evoked visions of emperors and royalty. The opulent buildings, temples, palaces, and pagodas touched the heavens, stirring amazement within Peiling's soul.

As she weaved through the bustling streets, the diverse array of people from all corners of the world left her mesmerized. The scent of exotic spices and incense mingled in the air, intoxicating her senses. The eastern terminal of the Silk Road had brought together a tapestry of cultures. Languages, sounds, colors, and smells intermingled harmoniously. In the heart of the city, the main square twisted into the form of the Big Dipper, an astronomical calendar etched into the paved stones, guiding the movements of time and destiny.

The Cien Temple complex, adorned with lavish hues of autumn, stood as a testament to the city's grandeur. Within its walls, Peiling stood transfixed by the giant Wild Goose Pagoda that seemed to stretch towards the heavens.

This magnificent structure, housing the sacred scriptures brought back from India, seemed to her to defy gravity. The figurines of the Gautama Buddha gracefully adorned both the inside and outside walls, reminding her of her own spiritual journey.

The temple's sprawling gardens embraced Peiling with their abundance, a stark contrast to the arid highlands of her home. Lotus trees, cherry blossoms and thriving orchards created a vibrant oasis, breathing life into her new surroundings. Monolithic stele stones etched with Confucian virtues and decorated with intricate animal illustrations stood in the gardens, fostering a sense of harmony and tranquility.

As Peiling settled into her new life, her unparalleled talent as a rider propelled her towards her destiny. Serving her apprenticeship as a polo player and courtier at the temple, commissioned by one of the most powerful families in Shaanxi Province, she found herself competing in matches between rival polo families of immense significance. Fortunes were made and lost with the outcomes of these contests, where Peiling's skills promised victory and success.

Her days began at dawn and ended at dusk, consumed by rigorous riding training, taking care of the horses, and tending to the flourishing fruit trees and gardens. Guided by the Buddhist monks in her spiritual growth and education, every step she took was infused with wisdom and enlightenment. Despite the demanding nature of her new life, Peiling cherished the opportunity. Becoming a skilled polo player was her path to glory and fame, a chance to break the boundaries that constrained women. In a profession where gender held no relevance, Peiling's determination burned bright.

Peiling always marveled at the vibrant green grass of the training quadrangle, as well as the colorful banners and ornate columns of the roofed cloister surrounding it. Topped with bright red earthenware tiles, the courtyard looked particularly picturesque on ordinary days, with the banners gently swaying in the morning breeze, as if waving their approval. However, on this specific day, the twenty sixth of January fifteen fifty six, an eerie stillness hung in the air, apart from the usual reverberating commands of her instructor.

The morning's lesson focused on dressaging the horses, guiding them to reverse effortlessly and dart from side to side. However, mere minutes into the session, the instructor abruptly ceased barking orders and fell silent. In the distance, a rumble began to build, growing louder until it reached a deafening crescendo. The entire quadrangle shook relentlessly, echoing like thunder, while the air itself seemed to vibrate with waves of destruction. With a sudden, violent jolt, the ground beneath Peiling's feet started undulating, resembling a tempestuous sea. The graceful horses bellowed in fear, losing their footing, and throwing their riders to the ground. The once mighty pillars of the cloister cracked and splintered, unable to withstand the force of the shaking earth. Bright red terracotta tiles cascaded from the rooftop, shattering upon impact with the ground.

Clutching the grass for dear life, Peiling felt as though she were tossed and turned by a wild bucking horse. The ground defied gravity, testing the limits of her endurance. Through trembling lips, she whispered prayers to her dragon guardian deity for forgiveness and pleaded for its help, fearing the collapse of her family's clay Yaodong home that could bury them alive.

The city itself seemed to roar with anguish as walls crumbled, the grand Wild Goose Pagoda sagged, and its towering presence diminished. The monstrous earthquake unleashed its wrath upon the land, tearing apart mountains and forming deep crevices. Rivers changed their courses, causing immense flooding, while candles and fires danced like malevolent fireflies, igniting relentless infernos. The earth transformed, reshaping the once-familiar landscapes. Hills violently rose and valleys sank, quickly becoming gaping chasms. Streams erupted from the dry ground, carving new gullies and structures that once stood tall succumbed to the relentless shaking. Huts, houses, temples, and city walls crumbled to dust, leaving shattered remnants of their former glory. Even the ancient stone steles, markers of an ancient civilization, lay broken in pieces.

As the tremors finally subsided, Peiling found herself miraculously alive, grateful for being in the open when the quake began. However, a sinking feeling consumed her heart as she realized that her family had not been as fortunate. The hillside where their community lived was now a pile of rubble and despair, a tragic mix of clay, mud, and limbs.

Amidst the chaos, the people of Chang'an and Shaanxi Province mourned their losses. Funeral pyres lit up the sky to honor the lost. Survivors began the arduous task of rebuilding their shattered lives. The Great Wild Goose Pagoda stood as a testament to the quake's power, having lost three entire stories. However, the black obsidian statue of the Traveling Buddha remained steadfast atop its granite pedestal, gazing upon the Cien Temple grounds with a compassionate gaze, symbolizing hope, and resilience in the face of tragedy.

In a matter of days, the already shaken populace found terror once again as a magnificent comet blazed across the night sky. Half the size of the moon, its fiery tail resembled a blazing torch. This celestial spectacle foretold more calamity and announced the impending arrival of the Four Perils, instilling dreadful predictions in the hearts of those who looked skyward. The burning star dragon, along with the devastating earthquake, became a portent of doom—a dire consequence of humanity's transgression.

Passage Four.

Once More Unwelcome.

Communities, their faith, and courage faltering, made the agonizing decision to forsake their once-revered protector, the Culebre dragon. Over generations, attitudes towards this mystical creature had shifted and now, emboldened, and unscrupulous vagabonds brazenly roamed, hunting the dragon with the sole intent of stealing its enchanted jewel.

Heart heavy with sorrow at this newfound rejection, the Culebre dragon ascended into the heavens once more, setting its course westward. Guided by the ethereal comet traversing the celestial expanse, the dragon looked down with sadness upon superstitious travelers venturing along the Silk Road, their paths winding through the treacherous Himalayan plateau, leading towards the enchanting lands of Europe.

While Peiling continued her ascent to polo stardom, the Culebre dragon left her and the Chinese people behind forever, just as its fellow castaways had done long ago. After years of relentless searching, it found peace upon returning to Europe, embraced by the comforting landscape of Wales, a nation proudly adorned with the emblem of the red dragon. Nestled under the watchful gaze of Mount Snowdon, it discovered serenity amidst the green valleys, lush forests, and murmuring brooks—a land steeped in the legends of Merlin and King Arthur. Now known as Cinaed Drake, it thrived in this Celtic realm as an artisan, renowned for its ethereal sculptures depicting the nation's revered emblem—the dragon. Crafted from bronze and carved from blue granite, these masterpieces adorned art galleries around the world.

Seeking solace within its mountain dwelling, which served as both residence and workshop, fiery smoke billowed from its metal forges. Enveloped in a state of secluded bliss, it concealed itself, its true form hidden from the prying eyes of the world. Only when the Culebre weaved a cloak of mist and ethereal fog around the mountain did it venture into the skies, soaring undetected, reveling in the liberating embrace of the heavens and anonymity.

Passage Five.

Revelry, Acceptance, and Hope.

Despite the comfort of seclusion, there were moments when Cinaed felt compelled to brave the outside world and travel to London, the vibrant capital of England. Situated within the swanky district of Mayfair, they owned a prestigious gallery displaying their dragon sculptures with pride.

When Cinaed found themselves in London, courage surged within their being, prompting them to embrace the city's delights. Donning their finest clothes adorned with vibrant colors borrowed from the rainbow, they cast aside their shyness and embraced the exhilarating nightlife. Their destination: the celebrated Heaven Nightclub, a subterranean haven where alternative lifestyles flourished, and people embraced individuality.

As Cinaed stepped into the club, the thunderous rhythms reverberating through the foundations of the railway station above grabbed at their soul. A mesmerizing light show danced across the room, intertwining colors in enchanting patterns. Bolts of lightning darted across the space, echoing the dragon's long-lost ability to conjure electric currents and invoking ancient power.

In this mesmerizing ambiance and amidst the pulsating energy of the dance club, a sense of unity and acceptance enveloped Cinaed, washing away past doubts. Their ethereal beauty halted club-goers in their tracks, entranced by their grace as they glided through the crowd.

Every eye followed Cinaed's hypnotic movements, their allure radiating undeniable magnetism. It was as if the air itself held its breath, intoxicated by their presence. In this sanctuary of self-expression, the dragon found profound belonging, reminiscent of ancient days surrounded by communal love and its eternal soulmate Hathor on Izbeckia.

In that moment, a question lingered. Would they ever reunite and retrace their steps through the vast expanse of space, gliding through nebulae and star clusters, back to their ancestral home? Contemplating the possibilities, their mind brimmed with hope and wonder.

"One day", Cinaed whispered, a tear meandering down their cheek.

STORY FOUR.

THE KITSUNÉ FOX.

Passage One.

The Kitsuné.

J apan boasts an awe-inspiring tapestry of volcanoes, towering-primordial forests, and misty mountains. This chain of isolated and mystifying islands, nestled amidst the embrace of bountiful seas, creates a breathtaking backdrop that captures the imagination.

Within the depths of Japan's rich folklore, lies a treasure trove of enchanting tales, woven with the threads of dragon kings, mischievous water-imps, ethereal lunar animal spirits and the miraculous birth of a boy from a peach. These narratives brim with imagination. They have a charm that is both captivating and sometimes chilling, making them unique in the annals of global storytelling. They reverberate with the essence of the country's ancient culture and traditions, deeply ingrained in the collective consciousness of its people.

Within these cherished traditions exists the enigmatic Kitsuné, a fox that garners as it ages an ever-expanding repertoire of paranormal abilities. These otherworldly creatures have the extraordinary ability to assume human form.

When transformed, they become smaller in stature, showing distinct Asian features with natural red hair. With muscular frames and remarkable agility, they boast an exquisite snow-white complexion, with sharp bewitching eyes that command attention.

Artisans and herbalists alike revere the Kitsuné, who serve as cunning yet loyal protectors, steadfast companions, and even passionate lovers. They are the keepers of secrets, guardians of wisdom and an embodiment of the intricate symbiosis between the human and spiritual worlds.

Passage Two.

The Guardian.

Akira Shaku lived in Kanagawa prefecture. Each day, he helped his family scrape out a living, toiling to support a modest existence. However, today marked a different path. Akira was slated to tend to the resplendent gardens of Kōtoku-in temple, a shrine nestled near the quaint village of Kamakura, where the venerable statue of Buddha majestically resides.

As the calm embrace of autumn rolled in, it was his job to prune back the Sakura cherry trees, preparing them for the icy tendrils of winter. With diligent hands, he would sweep away the fallen leaves, ensuring that the serene stream flowed unfettered through the gardens, meandering alongside the stone pathways caressing the lush beds of vibrant chrysanthemums.

His family's subsistence revolved around the beautiful shores of Lake Hamana, their simple boats landing the bountiful treasures beneath its glimmering surface. Along the banks, they gathered edibles and natural herbal remedies.

Akira's grandmother, a skilled practitioner of Kampo, the art of traditional Japanese medicine, would painstakingly dry, crush and amalgamate her cache, creating concoctions to sell at the bustling local market. This profound knowledge, passed down through generations, originated in the teachings of traveling monks who had settled in this corner of Japan. From potent ginseng to strong magnolia bark and even crushed beetles, she masterfully blended an array of ingredients. She formulated diverse powders and potions intended to remedy many common ailments.

For those plagued by pounding headaches, debilitating muscular pain or persistent acne, Akira's grandmother held the treatment, artfully wrapped within sachets of cloth, or snuggled within delicate ceramic bottles.

Once a week, she would journey to the market, where people eagerly sought her elixirs. They held faith in their ability to fortify the body, bestowing strength, and protection against the ravages of disease.

The Shaku's modest home, situated a short distance from the village, stood proudly along the shore of the lake. It was a typical Japanese Minka house. Gracefully fashioned from timber, it was topped with a sloping thatched roof of silver-grass and reeds.

A wooden engawa veranda encircled the home, while deep imposing eaves shielded it from the torrential winter rains and offered refuge from the sweltering summer sun. Within its interiors, the presence of traditional sliding fosuma doors and tatami mats fostered an atmosphere of simplistic elegance.

There was little to no privacy. He and his sister lived together with their mother, father, and doting grandmother.

The absence of a chimney caused smoke from the sunken hearth, known as the Irori, to linger momentarily before gracefully ascending through the roof. Ingeniously drying the reeds, it repelled undesired insects and pests. The Irori served as a focal point for the family, not solely for sharing meals and engaging in conversation but also as a cozy place to rest.

As the nights grew colder, Akira found comfort in the hearth's embrace, choosing it as his preferred place to sleep.

Akira napped a little longer, knowing he did not need to be at the temple until the monks returned from their prayers and rituals at 9 o clock. His family had left the house early after a simple breakfast of porridge, made from barley, acorns, fennel, and some wild berries.

However, a large red fox entering through the open door disrupted his plans to sleep in. The fox paused at his feet and growled menacingly. Terrified, Akira tried to shoo it away, but the growls grew louder and more threatening. Panicking, he backed away from the fox, which crouched and gradually inched closer.

In a rush of fear, Akira bolted for the door, grabbed his noragi winter coat and ran up the hill to the rear of the house. Much to his dismay, his snarling nemesis followed closely behind trapping him atop the hill, like a sheep dog working the herd. Akira darted from side to side, but to no avail. The fox was amazingly fast and incredibly agile. Finally, with no means to break free, Akira sat down on the hill and patiently waited for the fox to leave.

As the young Japanese boy gazed south over his home beyond the lake towards the Philippine Sea, he admired the beauty of the chinquapins, oak trees and camellia swaying in the ocean breeze. Hydrangea bushes donned gloriously in their autumnal blossoms of red, blue, and pink danced back and forth, partnered by the tall grasses that stretched to the sea and the reeds in the lake. The sun broke through wispy white clouds scattered across the sky, illuminating the bright fall day. Despite the stunning surroundings Akira knew he had to get to work. However, the fox remained unmoving, keeping a firm gaze fixed upon him.

Just as he was contemplating another escape attempt, a distant rumble caught his attention. The ground shook violently, throwing him around while he heard the cracking of trees and wood. The shaking continued relentlessly, and his fists clung to the stalks of grass, hoping the earth would not open and swallow him. Unwilling to face Jigoku, the Buddhist underworld, Akira prayed to his gods, informing them that he had lived a righteous life and was worthy of rebirth.

When the shaking finally ceased, he looked down towards his home and the lake, but all he saw were piles of fallen trees and debris. Tears welled up in his eyes. He hoped his family was safe. Although he wished to go down the hill, the fox remained resolute, growling louder than ever. On the lake, the family boats were nowhere in sight and his grandmother was not foraging like a badger at her favorite spot.

To his left, a dusky haze of dust rose from the village rooftops which no longer sparkled in the morning sun. Looking south, he caught a glimpse of the coast and Suruga Bay. Strangely the water appeared extremely far away. The beach unwilling to let go of its constant companion, had followed it out to the horizon. Overhead, loons, petrels, and shearwaters screeched and squawked as they fled inland, sensing an impending storm.

Fixated on the bay, Akira saw an intimidating wall of water, fifteen to twenty feet high, roaring back towards the coast. A gust of wind brushed against his face, and he heard the monastery's large gong being paddled frantically by a young monk, sounding the alarm.

From his vantage point, he saw the nightmare that befell every Japanese person living near the sea.

The furious ocean, writhing with venom, surged across the bay, mercilessly crushing the moored fishing boats. The trees resembled overmatched sentries struck by a colossal marauding battering ram. They fell to their knees, swept away from the very land they once guarded. Cast aside, they were powerless against the force that ravaged their fiefdom. As their shattered trunks crashed into the lake, the waves seized hold of the remnants of Akira's home, carrying the combined debris up and around the hill.

Perched on top of the summit, grief-stricken tears streamed down Akira's ashen face as the encroaching waters crept within a mere ten feet of his lonely position. The steadfast fox, never faltered in its gaze, ignoring the churning current below. As the water surged unrelentingly up the valley, it threatened to drown the village and the beautiful gardens of the nearby monastery. Overwhelmed by a sense of helplessness, Akira's desire to find his loved ones was thwarted by the implacable grasp of the immense tide and the resolute presence of the fox.

Eventually, after eight hours the water finally began to recede, leaving Akira unaware of the fate of his family or the monks. The fox, his mysterious savior, had vanished without a trace, leaving him to ponder who had sent this guardian to protect him.

Tragically, Akira never saw his mother or sister again. The torrent had swept them away, lost along with their boat. However, a small glimmer of hope remained. His father was found alive, battered, bruised, and clinging to the only tree left standing.

In a bewildering twist of fate, his grandmother miraculously appeared unscathed.

As a family, they had suffered immense losses, including the lake that had once sustained their livelihood, now destined to be a lifeless brackish backwater.

In deep mourning for his mother and sister, Akira prayed that they had reached Samsara, a blissful destination where they would be reborn. Together, the shattered family rebuilt their Minka home, this time on top of the hill, rather than in its shade. Moving forward, their focus shifted towards the practice of Kampo medicine and offering aid to their fellow citizens.

While the walls and the gardens of the monastery lay in ruins, a stoic stone statue of Buddha withstood the ravages of the pounding waves. In the aftermath of the earthquake and tsunami, the shrine took on a newfound spiritual significance and the monks gratefully accepted the help of the Shaku family.

Symbolizing their resilience and connection to the fox that saved Akira, the family now bore the emblem of Kitsuné. Together, they worked alongside the monks to restore the monastery gardens, allowing faithful visitors to marvel at the enduring statue of Buddha.

Spared by what seemed like divine authority, it now stood defiantly out in the open, overseeing the beauty of the cherry blossoms, rows of chrysanthemum and the meticulously tended herb garden of an incredibly old grandmother.

Passage Three.

The Family Tree.

Before Eighteen Sixty Eight, the Japanese people proudly bore the name of their clan or their humble peasant title. Yet, the late nineteenth century brought a revolution that swept across Japan, leading to the restoration of imperial rule under Emperor Meiji. With this transformation came a decree from the new leader, mandating that every citizen must register with a personal and a single-family name, as a symbol of unity and conformity.

The family had always been known as "Shaku," a revered and influential name in the Kamakura region. This name held a profound significance, as it embodied the values of compassion and diligent care for the sick. Though its origin denoted a humble "shoe" of the peasants, it stood as a beacon of respect and the dignity of hard work. However, due to the newly enacted law, Ichiro's great great grandfather had to choose a new name, one that would instill a sense of pride and embrace their family's history. Therefore, the name Kitzunezaki seemed a natural choice. A choice that paid homage to their heritage and their enduring connection with the foxes that still visited their hilltop home.

Perched atop the majestic hill, the ancestral home commanded a panoramic view of the briny lake and the channel that led to the vast expanse of the Philippine Sea. Rebuilt after the devastating tsunami, the house had undergone various renovations throughout the centuries. It now stood as a cherished sanctuary for Ichiro's grandparents.

The two-story home, constructed from sturdy oak, featured an intricately decorated roof with glazed round tiles. The first floor boasted a veranda, similarly, adorned with this resplendent stoneware and the interior exuded the essence of traditional Japanese design.

Encircled by a protective stone wall, the property sprawled across the entirety of the hill, accessible solely through an imposing gate held upright by a magnificent wooden archway.

Carefully carved cherry blossoms adorned the arch, while playful depictions of foxes danced in its midst. On either side of the winding driveway, Sakura trees stood proudly on parade, captivating the senses with their resplendent pink flowers during the enchanting arrival of spring. Nestled in the rear of the estate lay an opulent garden, embellished with chrysanthemums, hydrangeas and an array of flourishing vegetables and herbs, meticulously tended to by Ichiro's doting grandparents.

As a child, Ichiro Kitsunezaki spent countless days, reveling in the wonders of this vibrant garden, hiding from his mischievous siblings, and eagerly helping his grandparents with pruning and planting. In those cherished moments, enveloped by the enchanting fragrance of the flowers, his grandparents would regale him with tales of their storied family history, instilling in him a profound belief that he was uniquely special.

Passage Four. A Coming Together.

When Ichiro turned thirteen, his life underwent a seismic shift. The family moved to California, to seek new opportunities and expand the family business of Kampo herbal medicine. They made the difficult decision to uproot themselves from their homeland and embrace a new life in America.

Southern California, with its burgeoning Asian community and a growing interest in alternative medicine, presented a promising starting point for the Kitsunezaki's endeavors.

While they had been exporting some of their products to the United States for years, demand had recently surged. Ichiro's father bore the responsibility of ensuring that their family's Kampo products would occupy prominent spaces within health stores and pharmacies across America.

Upon their arrival, they found a home on a hill near a working farm in San Juan Capistrano.

At night they could hear coyotes howling,

breathe in the fragrant natural air and feel the ocean breeze blowing in from the Pacific. It was not too dissimilar from their home thousands of miles away and they quickly settled into the rhythm of American everyday life.

Ichiro approached his first day at Marco Forster Middle School with a mixture of nervousness and anticipation. While he had a good grasp of the English language and could hold a conversation, he could not help but wonder if he would be able to keep up with the other students when the subject matter became more technical. Making new friends was also a concern weighing on his mind.

Assigned a desk towards the back of the classroom, Ichiro found himself sitting near a large map of the world. As he glanced at it, he could not help but feel a pang of homesickness as he compared the size of Japan to the vastness of the United States. In that moment he missed his grandmother.

During the teacher's introductory remarks about the semester's curriculum, Ichiro listened attentively while placing a list of required supplies into his new backpack. The teenagers were all focused on the front of the class, except for a fellow student a few rows ahead. This dark-skinned boy repeatedly glanced around, staring at him. This was the first time Ichiro met Miles Cawtheray.

At morning recess, Ichiro chose to keep to himself and sat in the shade of a large eucalyptus tree by the side of the basketball court. To his surprise, Miles approached him accompanied by two friends - a blonde-haired girl named Sarah, and a dark-haired boy named Jose. Though Sarah and Jose stood nearby, their presence seemed protective, shielding Ichiro from prying eyes.

"How long have you been shifting?" Miles asked suddenly.

Caught off guard, Ichiro mumbled a response in Japanese.

Miles smiled and introduced himself, pointing to Sarah and Jose who followed suit.

"We all have abilities." Miles declared. "We thought we were the only ones in the school until you arrived today. What animal do you become.?" He inquired.

Ichiro remain silent, puzzled at how Miles was aware of his special gift.

"If you don't want to say that's fine," Miles continued, "but I hoped we could be friends.

Sarah here likes to swim. In fact, she swims just like a dolphin." Miles explained, winking cheekily.

"Jose likes to fly and truthfully, he soars just like an eagle. And as for me, I am agile like a cat and see things, not only in the dark, but what others may not see." Miles grinned.

Ichiro hesitated before timidly responding.

"I am clever, cunning, and aloof. Just like a fox."

And so, the "Quad Squad" was born - a tight-knit group of inseparable friends.

They supported each other in their academic pursuits, attending each other's events and lending help with homework assignments. Whether it was Miles playing baseball, Sarah displaying her swimming skills, Ichiro competing in chess or Jose excelling in the high jump, the other three squad members were always there to cheer them on. They spent their weekends together, appreciating moments when they could reveal their true selves to one another.

One of their favorite things to do was to go with Sarah to the ocean. As she gleefully splashed in the water, Jose would soar above squawking, diving, and dancing with her as she jumped through the waves. Meanwhile Ichiro and Miles playfully tussled like a cat and a dog on the sandy shore, occasionally venturing to climb the large rocks to watch their friend's ballet. While Miles was cautious to keep his distance from the water, Ichiro fearlessly darted in and out of the surf, happily chomping at the bubbling foam, yelping, and jumping with joy

Bound by a powerful sense of solidarity, the Quad Squad vowed to never keep secrets from each other and to safeguard their unique abilities from inquisitive outsiders.

Months later, Miles revealed the existence of an extraordinary mercurial sphere found by his archaeologist Uncle to his friends. Miles described how it affected him deeply, while having no impact on the other people present.

Explaining his experience, Miles shared that when he had touched the sphere, an extraordinary story unfolded before his eyes. Like a vivid trailer for a movie, flashes of the past cascaded through his mind. He saw the enigmatic sight of a distant planet with six majestic moons, inhabited by melancholic homogeneous gray-beings. These aliens embarked on a journey and left their crippled vessel, descending to earth in silvery balls of fire.

The surreal visions continued to captivate Miles's imagination. He envisioned kings and queens of ancient times, their palms adorned with ethereal purple crystals. Inexplicably humans transformed into a menagerie of creatures. birds, wolves, cats and even crocodiles. Supernatural beings hurled bolts of lightning as if they were javelins, while a circular globe displayed a bygone Earth teeming with radiant lights and mysterious symbols.

Eager to uncover the secrets hidden within, Miles spoke with conviction, "We must find out what is in that sphere! I think it could be a spaceship." He believed wholeheartedly that the sphere held the key to explaining their uniqueness.

In that moment, a thought entered the Quad Squad's collective mind.

They were about to embark on an extraordinary treasure hunt.

STORY FIVE.

SOBEK. THE CROCODILE GOD.

Passage One.

The Nile River.

In a small village nestled along the banks of the upper Nile, thirty miles from the majestic Aswan dam, people go about their daily routines. Life here revolves around the mighty river from which they fish and gather water to irrigate their crops.

The humble dwellings of the villagers stand in proximity to the ancient temple of Crocodopolis. This sacred sanctuary houses the remnants of a forgotten era, where echoes of beliefs linger within its weathered walls. The villagers pay homage to Sobek, a deity believed to have descended from the sky to preside over this sacred ground with mesmerizing mystery. They place fragrant flowers at his feet against a backdrop of hieroglyphs, alongside offerings of freshly poured goat's blood as tokens of reverence.

A god of immense power and ferocity, Sobek's statue bears his fearsome countenance. It is eight feet tall and combines the exquisite craftsmanship of a humanoid figure adorned with a crocodile's head. Within this amalgamation, his razor-sharp teeth gleam brilliantly in contrast to the greenish hue that graces his scaly skin. Enigmatic orbs of piercing intensity, his eyes look forward over powerful jaws. Specks of yellow dancing amidst a marbled jade captivate all who dare to stare. In this paradoxical worship, the people revere Sobek as the Lord of the River, a reputed philanderer, and a thief. The villagers pray to their god to subdue the monstrous crocodiles that lurk in the river, ensuring the safety of their homes and most importantly, their innocent children.

Passage Two.

Horror in Yosemite.

The tremors over the past two weeks had everyone at the ranger station on edge. Sam Dannett, a rugged and tanned man with shaggy blond hair and sharp handsome features, was a ranger who had worked in the park since graduating from UC Davis, where he studied land management. He felt uneasy, despite knowing that small quakes could ward off something more catastrophic.

The park was unusually quiet as he patrolled up to the Tuolumne River that morning. The birds were not singing and even the mule-deer, against the backdrop of the sharp snow-covered peaks, appeared restless while grazing in the meadow. His thoughts flooded back to that summer ten years ago when he had these same premonitions and the gruesome scene he discovered.

"Those poor German tourists!" He recalled.

Taking off his hat, Sam rubbed his face two-handed as if washing away the memory. He brushed his forehead with his sleeve and looked towards the campground.

He recalled the limbs torn and scattered around the campsite and headless torsos sitting in the branches of trees, macabrely dripping blood onto the ground. The stench of death and excrement hung heavy in the air. That pungent odor lingered vividly in his memory.

Of course, every person's first reaction was that a huge bear had gone on a rampage. But that amount of carnage was not the norm, and there were no tracks or signs of a black bear. At that time of year, bears tend to stay in the lower areas of the park.

The FBI forensic team found puncture wounds in many of the body parts, but none matched the bite from a bear. A bear certainly would have eaten what it killed, but investigators collected and accounted for most of the limbs of the victims.

The only missing organs from the deceased were the nutrient-rich livers and hearts. The coroner found that no tool or knife had cut their bodies. Instead, someone or something had simply ripped the limbs from their torsos, twisted and pulled them apart.

When the FBI performed forensic tests on the bite wounds, they concluded that the samples had to be tainted. They tested negative for bear and human DNA but showed they were reptilian in origin.

Unless dinosaurs were still roaming Yosemite, the FBI had no answers. The coroner was equally baffled and simply wrote the cause of death as "massive body trauma and dismemberment."

"Was it murder?" Everyone asked.

"Probably." But they had no leads.

FBI detectives aided by the park rangers, did a thorough investigation, closing the picnic area and scouring the entire area looking for clues. They checked all vehicles that had entered the park from surveillance camera footage. They interviewed all visitors to the park that day.

The potential suspects ranged from retired persons, midwestern families on vacation, day trippers, college kids at the park to tackle half dome and even a billionaire industrialist who was getting some rest and relaxation trekking the Sierra Nevada.

The detectives toiled for months, hoping for more information and leads, but nothing new materialized.

With no further evidence or suspects, the FBI closed the case and filed it away unsolved. No one, other than the killer, knew the whole story behind the death of Gunter Hitzelberger, his wife Astrid and their two young children, Karl, and Heidi.

Some years later, Sam was watching a nature show on television about the wildebeest migration across the Mara River in Africa. Sam was fascinated to watch the awaiting crocodiles ferociously attack, clamp down on their prey and roll violently, tearing away flesh and limbs. Everyone would think it crazy, but the idea of a creature like that existing in Yosemite seemed both unbelievable and frightening.

Passage Three. Marooned.

Ten thousand years ago, Sobek's pod was one of the last to leave the ship, moments before it left orbit to limp towards Izbeckia and home. His escape sphere had crash-landed in a wondrous landscape, its metallic shell bouncing across the surface of a grand river and sinking into the sandy shore. As he appeared from inside, his senses tingled with the exhilaration of new surroundings. The pristine beauty of the land stretching out before him was both captivating and daunting. The giant river was a remarkable sight, its clear waters colder and less viscous than those on his home planet. They flowed like an unstoppable army mirroring the cerulean sky above.

On the northeast side of him, a soaring range of sand dunes rose majestically. These yellow hills stood in stark contrast to the trees and foliage that garnished the valley floor. It was a tapestry of nature's handiwork, a portrait of a land unspoiled and resilient.

Venturing forward, his bare feet sank into the soft sand, leaving imprints that whispered tales of his otherworldly presence. The wind danced through the reed beds in the river, carrying ancient melodies and whispered of unfolding legends. The rustling of the tall grass joined forces with birdsong, creating a haunting symphony that both allured and cautioned him.

His escape pod held a trove of invaluable treasures. Within its mercurial shell lay an assortment of artifacts, each with a unique purpose. Among the cache were survival provisions, including a precious cylinder cradling liquid metal infused with microscopic machines.

These ethereal nanobots bestowed upon the Izbek the extraordinary ability to mend and regrow limbs, granting them immunity against disease and the potential for immortality. Also, Inside Sobek's sphere rested coveted crystals with potent energies and an enchanted amulet that worked in tandem. These remarkable gems granted Sobek and all Izbek an unprecedented means to harness the forces of nature. The Earth itself became their sacred conduit and playground. Cloaked in mastery over gravity, the Izbek tapped into the abundant energy sown within the Earth's magnetic field. With effortless grace, they conjured tempests and tamed the weather to their every whim. Lightning bolts performed a breathtaking spectacle at their fingertips, while fireballs radiated danger and wonder from their palms.

The might of the Izbek extended far beyond meteorological manipulation. With a mere gesture, mountains trembled, and towering granite blocks succumbed to their command. A subtle movement of their arms could lay waste to entire armies, leaving nothing but devastation in their wake. Since their unexpected arrival on Earth, the Izbek castaways skillfully harnessed their extraordinary shape-shifting abilities to blend in with indigenous tribes, concealing their true identities. Assuming the form of human beings and fearsome creatures, they wove a complex tapestry of power and control. As a testament to their glorious home world, the Izbek worked hand in hand with their supplicants, shaping majestic civilizations that would endure in the annals of time. Revered as deities, they erected magnificent pyramids, holy temples, and megalithic creations, leaving no culture untouched by their guidance. Along the banks of the Nile River, Sobek, the crocodile god, created the sacred grounds of Egypt where he molded humanity, illuminating their path from nomadic insignificance to the dazzling promise of the future. However, as the sands of time shifted, the flickering light of rescue faded from Sobek's mind, leaving him resigned to a permanent life on Earth. In ancient times, he bathed in the open adoration of the masses, freely displaying his extraordinary powers. Now however, mankind's emerging enlightenment forced him to mask his true identity. Striving to keep power, he moved through history like a phantom gracefully pirouetting around the delicate dance of life. He shifted and transformed, mimicking death, and adopting the visage of his own descendants, ensuring the seamless transfer of wisdom and wealth across generations. In the wake of global power shifting westward, Sobek migrated away from the lands where his grand temples once soared.

Passage Four.

The Horrific Trade.

In eighteen twenty-five Sobek, now known as Martin Krugler, arrived in the United States, and settled in the bustling town of New Bedford Massachusetts. With a population of around twenty thousand, this vibrant coastal town held a unique distinction - it boasted the greatest concentration of American wealth, all thanks to the precious commodity of whale oil.

As the demand for whale oil soared with the ever-growing population, it sparked history's most dangerous and thrilling hunts. Brave men would embark on voyages that spanned half the world, sailing in small boats and facing down the largest animals on earth.

Harpoons would cruelly pierce the majestic creatures' bodies, turning the waves a macabre crimson. Whalers brutally hacked these magnificent beasts to pieces, solely driven by greed, their hearts deaf to the echoing screams of the dying animals.

Though horrific to understand, this dark and gruesome industry was precisely why Martin Krugler came to America at a time when controlling this murderous trade meant great wealth and power.

Krugler saw an opportunity for technical innovation but also financial success. Krugler's fleet had the most advanced and fastest ships, with weapons forged from legendary Damascus steel. Manned by expert captains and harpooners, his vessels sailed the seas with unparalleled efficiency.

However, when prospectors discovered crude oil in Pennsylvania, Krugler sensed the winds of change. He foresaw the impending decline of the whaling industry and decided to become a significant player in the nascent petroleum market.

Leaving behind the once treacherous seas, he transferred most of his wealth. He founded the Sobek Corporation, a name reminiscent of his past glory.

With the acquisition and sale of a refinery on Long Island, he swiftly became a major partner in the emerging Standard Oil company. Through strategic investments in stocks, he earned the nickname "The Wizard of Wall Street." And by the late eighteen nineties, after transferring money to his future self, he had amassed a fortune worth billions.

Throughout the twentieth century, he continued to buy small oil-producing firms and refineries. Today, the Sobek Corporation is the world's most influential energy company.

Krugler once again held sway over the civilized world, reminiscent of ancient times in Crocodopolis on the Nile River.

Passage Five. The Thirst for Power.

Martin Krugler, the CEO of Sobek corporation, loomed like a vicious dictator, his influence stretching across the globe as he controlled a sizable part of the world's fossil fuel supply. Krugler's evil tendrils captured production facilities, fracking operations and mineral extraction plants scattered across multiple continents. He dictated the prices of coal, oil, and natural gas, pivotal in shaping the intricate web of global energy politics. He could hold the world to ransom at the drop of a hat if he so desired.

Nevertheless, Krugler's reach did not extend into the rare earth mineral industry, a sector where Krugler saw a potential bonanza.

These minerals were invaluable in producing cell phones and electric vehicles, both industries poised for exponential growth. Determined to seize this opportunity, Krugler would go to extreme lengths, even unabashedly engaging in conflicts with nation-states, just to secure a fraction of the exotic metal market for himself.

However, the German government, mired in concerns about environmental consequences, considered denying Sobek corporation mining rights in Saxony. Sobek recently bought land in this region to extract crucial minerals like Cerium and Neodymium. Not only do these elements play a vital role in generating the strongest permanent magnets, with applications ranging from levitation to electricity generation, but they also may lead to technologies creating super sonic land travel.

Krugler could not allow this potentially lucrative opportunity to slip through the greedy fingers of the Sobek corporation.

After leaving his office in New York, Krugler traveled to Yosemite in search of Gunter Hitzelberger, an influential environmental crusader, with the ear of German politicians. Gunter's vehement opposition to mining rare earth metals due to their destructive effects on the natural environment, was the reason that the Sobek Corporation's European mining ventures had stalled. Gunter and his family were vacationing in the National Park, enjoying the serenity of nature.

Hitzelberger expressed disgust at the exploitation of the environment in the name of progress and he, along with his wife and children, paid the ultimate price for his conviction.

Fully aware that convincing Gunter to shift his stance would be a waste of time, Krugler opted for a far more sinister approach. Instead of trying to convert the environmentalist to his cause, he made the unthinkable decision.

Krugler butchered the entire Hitzelberger family, demonically turning their idyllic campsite into a tableau of carnage and blood. Then with a calm demeanor, the billionaire feasted and returned to the East Coast, leaving no remorse behind.

Krugler's success in business derived from his shrewd ability to mask his true nature and his willingness to maneuver on the fringes of legality. Employing underhanded tactics such as bribery and buyouts, he effortlessly ended any competition daring enough to challenge his dominance. His goal was to transform Sobek into an indomitable conglomerate by tightly controlling the world's energy supply, cementing his position as the supreme ruler of that realm.

As if echoing his ancient Egyptian incarnation as Sobek, the revered crocodile god, presiding over this kingdom. Krugler's insatiable hunger for power knew no bounds. In the past, during the days of his divine rule, he had mercilessly wielded the awe-inspiring Izbekian technology, provided by his amulet and his celestial sphere. However, the fleeting remnants of that power had long diminished, propelling Krugler on a constant search to find a lost sphere carrying power crystals and harness their unparalleled strength.

Returning to his opulent office, overlooking Manhattan—the heart of his empire—Krugler could hardly hold his excitement after opening an email from one of his corrupt government contacts. This inconspicuous message signaled that his coveted, ultimate quest would once again lead him back to California.

A trench-digging tractor on a construction site in San Diego had struck something large and extremely hard, causing the hydraulics to fail. As the crew cautiously dug around the object with shovels, they discovered an astonishing shiny sphere, approximately eight feet long, that remained unblemished, devoid of scratches or marks except for four peculiar symbols arranged in a pentagonal shape. To their surprise, the metallic object was unexpectedly lightweight and like nothing else they had ever seen.

Passage Six.

The Golden State.

Krugler hurriedly left New York and made his way to La Guardia Airport. He boarded one of the Sobek Corporation's private jets bound for California. Immediately upon arrival, he rushed to the building site where he found groups of scientists rushing around like disturbed ants, perplexed, and confused. With a simple phone call to an influential friend, he was granted access to the site. Approaching the ancient sphere, Krugler gently pressed his palm against its symbols, causing the top to dissolve into nothingness.

As the lid disappeared, the interior revealed itself to be identical to the vessel he had boarded thousands of years ago. A surge of greed and nostalgia washed over him, the corners of his mouth curling up into a satisfied smile. As he ingested some of the Liquid Metal and allowed the nanites to flow through his veins, he realized that he was about to claim his former glory of the distant past. His Amulet pulsated with revived vigor and purple lightning crackled between his fingers. Grinning, he knew that he could once again manipulate humanity, shaping and molding mankind's development from a position of power.

STORY SIX.

THE PANTHER CHILD.

Passage One.

*Millennia ago, in
the Nile Valley.*

In a lush valley along the banks of a great river in what would one day be known as Egypt, a group of Paleo humans abruptly stopped their daily activities to gaze at a streak of light cutting across the darkening sky. Mesmerized, they watched as the fireball vanished behind the hills in the east where the setting sun cast long shadows. Though curiosity tugged at their hearts, the encroaching night and lurking predators kept them rooted in the safety of their surroundings. They looked at each other and smiled. The celestial phenomenon was a sign, a promise of good fortune for their upcoming hunt in the grasslands beside the river.

On a sandy slope nearby, the Izbek survivor of the crash stood alongside her escape pod, nestled beside a solitary palm tree. Peering out into the moonlit landscape, she contemplated her next move, her vision obscured by the veils of night. With the dawn hours away, she sought refuge within the protective confines of her pod, wondering if any of her fellow castaways had found their way to this place. Holding onto her amulet, she realized that most of her kind had also landed nearby. As the first light of dawn bathed the valley in its gentle glow, she watched a group of bipedal figures below engaged in a primal dance of survival. These hunters, displaying a fervor befitting predators, closed in on a majestic animal with golden horns, plunging sharp sticks into its flesh until it fell with a bellow of agony. Witnessing the ensuing violence, she felt a mixture of shock and exhilaration, prompting her to silently trail the hunters to their settlement crafted from earth and sticks.

The hunters returned triumphant to their camp, dragging the carcass of the massive antelope amid jubilant cheers from the females and children. Amidst this display of primal triumph, Bastet, as she came to be known, recognized the abundance of the land and the promise it held for survival. Embracing the form of the bipedal creatures that roamed the valley and donning the powerful shape of the leopard, she blended seamlessly into the tapestry of this thriving ecosystem.

Utilizing her amulet, Bastet sought out her fellow survivors who had also assumed human forms, some taking on avatars resembling the creatures of the land and sky. Together, they harnessed their ancient wisdom and unique abilities to guide the humans in creating a prosperous civilization amidst the splendor of the Nile valley. Temples rose in grandeur, pyramids pierced the sky and palaces stood as monuments to their shared legacy, intricately aligned with the celestial patterns of the stars above.

While the years flowed like the river, civilizations rose and fell as humanity charted its course towards enlightenment. Bastet, ever mindful of her true nature and the passage of time, withdrew into solitude within the confines of a temple-pyramid, assuming the mantle of a revered feline warrior goddess, a guardian of the sun. From her sanctuary, she watched as generations came and went like clouds drifting across the sky, shaping the tapestry of existence with their fleeting lives.

As the influence of the Izbek waned and human civilization flourished, Bastet navigated the shifting currents of time, concealing her identity and embracing anonymity amongst the simple folk of the south. Through the ages, she assumed various guises, witnessing the evolution of faith, belief, and the enduring spirit of humanity, all while silently awaiting the return of her kin from across the galaxy and the rescue that lingered on the horizon.

Passage Two.

Centuries later. The Disappearance.

Miles Cawtheray lived in Huddersfield West Yorkshire with his mother Edith. She had a free-spirited nature and would captivate her son with enthralling and mythical stories. She often pointed at people and proclaimed, "there goes a shifter!"

When Miles inquired further, she would cryptically inform him, that he would come to understand in time.

"You'll get the sight," she would assure him.

"Shifters, little people, and those not of this world are special and they help more than they hinder. Most are good but some...." Her words invariably trailed off. "Well, all in good time," and she always left it at that, but promised she would explain to him when the time came.

Miles was only five when he came home from Woodhouse school that frigid night. As always, he had left the old Victorian building, that looked more like a prison than a place of learning and headed home. He remembered that it was already dark, as the sun sets early in Yorkshire that time of year. The date was December twenty second, the winter solstice. and he was looking forward to opening presents on Christmas morning.

He walked alone and along Ashbrow road flanked on the left by a dense wood and a stone wall covered in moss. The trees had long shed their leaves, while their limbs like fingers clutching at air, where swaying in what was a quite strong winter breeze. Thousands of fallen leaves littered the path and he could still remember that earthy smell of mulch kicked up by his Wellington boots.

Simba, his giant tabby cat, never failed to surprise him on his way home from school. Every day like clockwork, she would leap onto the wall and follow him home.

Although he never really remembered her as a kitten, she had always been a constant companion. When he was home either his mother or Simba were always there. Strangely however, he could not remember them ever being together at the same time, but their individual presence was enough for him to feel protected.

Simba was no ordinary cat. She had a fearless spirit, one that terrified the neighbors gentle German Shepherd who always avoided her. This was extremely amusing from a bystanders' point of view.

As a skilled hunter, she would kill and eat the annoying starlings that always filled their roof at dusk.

Whenever Miles would tell people about Simba, they would always be amazed.

However, on that cold December day, Simba was no where to be seen. Having trudged home, he found the entire house empty and deserted. Wide-opened doors welcomed the biting chill of winter inside. Instead of a crackling fire in the living room, all that remained were cold unfeeling ashes. His Mother was conspicuously absent, leaving Miles with a growing sense of alarm.

Running into the back garden, hoping to find comfort and see her tending to the soil and plants, he was met only by the freezing cold breeze. Adding to the mystery, the laundry was still hanging on the line after nightfall and the slot to the coal cellar was propped open. This was perplexing, as he knew the coal man had already made his delivery for the month. He remembered feeding his horse.

As Miles peered down into the darkness, there appeared to be a smattering of blood and some prints on the ground. He recognized the unmistakable paw print of a large cat and the imposing tracks of a large dog, far larger than the pet next door. The absence of Simba and his mother filled him with fear and overwhelming loneliness. Tears welled up in his eyes as he sprinted to his neighbors' house, desperately hoping to find his mother.

The Smiths, longtime family friends, offered reassurance, believing his mother would soon reappear.

"She will turn up," they told him, but once they returned him home and saw the bloodstains, they promptly contacted the police.

What had happened and where were Simba and his mother?

Passage Three.

The Winter Solstice.

Ulf Cadman once known as Wepwawet in ancient times was the Izbekian enforcer and assassin. Ulf knew that there comes once in a generation instances where he needed to personally intervene and eradicate a threat. Thus, it was on a freezing winter's day that he found himself in a desolate wool manufacturing town in West Yorkshire. A bitter-cold place, its daunting mill chimneys poised like satanic sentries against a backdrop of somber gray, the air thick with fog that stank of soot.

This night on the winter solstice, an extraordinary event was about to unfold. A young cat changeling was about to appear for the very first time. An extremely rare shapeshifter that had the extraordinary ability to peer into the future. This shifter would be capable of unraveling the true intentions of the ancient Izbek, endangering their unchallengeable dominion here on earth.

Ulf Cadman, Wepwawet, intended to kill Miles Cawtheray.

However, he had underestimated this child's protective mother who had discovered Ulf lying in ambush. The scene of a voracious wolf attacking a female puma protecting her cub had played out many times before in wilderness areas around the world. However, it had never occurred in the frigid coal cellar of a small mill-terrace house and never with such ferocity.

Flinging each other violently into the walls, the combatants created a tornado of black dust fueled by slashing claws and snarling jaws. The cacophony of growls and caterwauls from the wolf and the wild cat resonated loudly around that dark-claustrophobic room. The whirling ball of fury spilled out into the garden and along a once quiet lane to a wooded thicket. Battered, bruised and bleeding heavily, both animals were limping and close to exhaustion.

Summoning extra strength, Ulf finally managed to throw the cat violently against a tree.

As the cat lay unconscious, the wolf followed up with a crunching death-bite to its head.

Ulf Cadman killed Edith Cawtheray, Miles's courageous mother. He dumped her carcass onto Bradford Road, a main thoroughfare where many pets had perished under the wheels of passing cars and busses.

Ulf, however, did not leave the battle unscathed. Edith had left her mark. His nose and cheek had deep scratches caused by her claws. She had broken his hind leg in two places, and he had lost part of his right ear. Staring down at his wounds and the puddles of blood, turned solid by the freezing Yorkshire air, he lamented that the problem of Miles Cawtheray would have to wait for another day.

Passage Four.

Metamorphosis.
The Panther.

When he was ten years old, accompanied by his beloved uncle, who had adopted him after his mother's disappearance, Miles Cawtheray moved to the sun-kissed shores of California. In the Golden State, time knew no bounds and by the age of thirteen, Miles had grown taller than most teenagers. He had a slender and sinewy build with jet black curls crowning his confident head. Inherited from his father's lineage, his maple skin added a touch of exotic allure. He proudly proclaimed his nationality as "Afro-British," a testament to his multifaceted heritage, from the sprawling plains of Rhodesia to the rugged industrial valleys of Yorkshire.

But it was not just Miles' handsome features that caught attention. His unique running style always brought a beaming smile to his uncle's face. A spectacle of athleticism and sheer determination, his arms pumped up and down like steam pistons, as if he were striving to outpace his very own legs. This young lad had an insatiable curiosity, an insurmountable thirst for understanding and unraveling the mysteries of the world.

Though endowed with many talents, Miles often wondered how his uncle would react if he were to discover his hidden abilities.

It was on the fateful night when his mother vanished without a trace that these latent powers awakened, stirred to life by the radiant light of the full moon. He was torn from slumber by a haunting nightmare. In this dream, a terrifying wolf-like creature stalked him through a dense-night-shrouded forest. The youngster awoke to an astonishing sight.

Trembling, he stood on all fours, his muscles rippling beneath the lunar glow. His hands contorted into fierce claws, an intimidating silhouette mirroring that of a snarling predatory panther poised to pounce upon his innocent Pokémon poster decorating the wall.

Once skeptical of his mother's tales, dismissing them as mere whimsical stories spun to entertain a wide-eyed child, Miles now had no doubt that they were true.

As his mother had promised, he was indeed special, a chosen one of supernatural descent. With focused determination, he mastered the skill of transformation, no longer bound by the whims of the moonlight. With "the sight" bestowed upon him, as his mother had promised, he could now point out his fellow shapeshifters.

Nevertheless, this newfound ability did not come without its dangers. Miles found himself facing opposition from those who valued solitude and anonymity, perceiving his presence as a menacing intrusion into their secretive realm. This shadowy world promised both peril and excitement as Miles readied himself to delve into the mysteries of his ancestry and explore the depths of his abilities.

STORY SEVEN.

COJICO. THE JAGUAR.

Passage One.

A legend stalks the land.

I n the depths of the verdant Mexican wilderness, amidst the towering canopies and secrets whispered by the ancient trees, lived a deity of magnificent power and awe. Cojico, the fabled shapeshifter jaguar god, descended upon the earth in a blazing ball of fire, heralded by crackling lightning and thunderous roars that reverberated through the very fabric of existence. With every step he took, the earth quivered beneath his mighty paws, as if paying homage to his divine presence.

As he prowled through his mysterious realm, the air stirred with anticipation, carrying with it the mingling scents of damp earth, wildflowers and the faint hint of ozone, a reminder of the electric fury he commanded. Lithe and graceful, his feline form was a fluid symphony of movement, muscles rippling beneath his obsidian- black fur like serpents coursing through the undergrowth. But it was his piercing emerald gaze that captured the hearts and souls of the Zapotec people, for within those eyes flickered the ancient wisdom of the gods.

High above in the boundless heavens, Cojico transforms into a majestic, winged serpent. He embarks on a celestial journey, navigating among the swirling storm clouds that populate the expansive sky. With every breath that escapes him, a verdant forest bursts forth, its emerald foliage whispering enchantments into the wind. The ethereal tears that escape his countenance cascade down, intertwining to form rivers that meander gracefully into vast lakes, glistening like molten silver. And through his gaze, the intricate wonders of the natural world unfold, as creatures of awe-inspiring diversity evolve, a testament to his boundless power.

Passage Two.

The Jaguar God.

Centuries ago, Cojico's escape pod careened away from his fellow Izbek castaways, hurtling through the clouds until it crash-landed on a precipitous ridge. From this vantage point, the extraterrestrial shapeshifter beheld a stunning fertile valley, cradled between the formidable Sierra Madre del Sur and the Sierra Madre de Oaxaca. Within this bountiful region, tribes of humans lived, their territories teeming with life and marked by relentless battles over hunting grounds and territorial boundaries.

In this wondrous landscape, an array of majestic creatures thrived. Mammoth, ancient horses and turkeys roamed freely, while the bizarre and mysterious Glyptoda, an enormous armadillo-like animal the size of a modern-day car, lumbered through the woods and across the valley floor. Large predatory cats, their eyes ablaze with primal hunger, stealthily pursued their prey, reveling in the abundance.

Cojico, gratefully acknowledging his luck, discovered that this land provided him with everything he needed for survival, a haven blessed with a mild climate, winding rivers, babbling streams, verdant woods, and lush meadows. He assumed the guise of a human, as well as donning the majestic form of the jaguar, the forest's apex predator and the most beautiful creature he had ever seen.

Harnessing his immense powers, Cojico deployed his wisdom and the dedicated labor of his subjects to forge a prosperous civilization where he could live comfortably and await rescue. The magnificent Monte Alban temple materialized, an awe-inspiring testament to Cojico's ingenuity and devotion. Standing resolute in the heart of the Zapotec nation, this grand edifice featured a pyramid that echoed the architectural marvels on his home world, Izbeckia. Seen from the heavens above, these structures formed an intricate tapestry, perfectly aligned with the constellation Pleiades, a celestial homage ingrained within their foundations.

Awaiting rescue and for the Izbek to return, Cojico withdrew into a secluded life within the temple-pyramid where he became a revered figure - a god and holy man, born and reborn throughout the annals of time. From his lofty perch he bore witness to the ebb and flow of countless generations, their lives as transient as raindrops falling from the sky.

In the beginning, Cojico stalked the land, his primal instincts guiding his hunts beneath the ancient canopy. Over time, however, his devout followers showered him with offerings of fruits, vegetables, and sacrificial animals, ensuring his sustenance and marking his divinity.

In repayment for their unwavering devotion, he bestowed upon them the gifts of mathematics, writing and the enigmatic art of calendrical notation. Under his rule and leadership, the Zapotecs thrived, even defying the might of the Aztec empire that yearned to conquer their lands.

In the heat of battle, Cojico commanded his warriors with an air of fierce determination. His form rippled and transformed into that of a ferocious jaguar, his obsidian and golden fur shimmering in the sunlight as he led his loyal soldiers into the heart of the conflict.

From his outstretched paw, bolts of lightning crackled and surged, striking down their foes with a display of unrivaled might. Explosive bursts of energy illuminated the battlefield, casting an ethereal purple light on the valiant warriors fighting alongside their leader.

To all would be conquerors, the message was clear. Under his watchful gaze, Cojico, the transforming jaguar-god, fiercely protected the land and the Zapotec people.

Passage Three.

The Amethyst.

Cojico, the marooned Izbek, always carried or wore a pentagonal silver amulet adorned with a purplish gemstone. The meticulously crafted metal setting, appeared to be alive, constantly moving and swirling with color. Within the depths of the Amethyst lay a captivating vortex of ever-changing light that held anyone who dared to gaze into it mesmerized and frozen in place.

With the Amulet in his possession Cojico was able to tap into its power, manipulating and harnessing energy with his thoughts. The mystical object enabled him not only to construct astonishingly grand palaces and temples but also to conjure bolts of lightning capable of toppling the very structures they had built and vanquish the armies of their enemies.

Passage Four.

In Search of Hope.

As time passed, Cojico, the once esteemed deity of the Zapotec nation, wondered if rescue would ever come. In Fifteen Forty Eight, he abandoned Mexico, taking on the identity of Archbishop Junipero Gattuso from the Diocese of Antequera. By securing passage on a gold-laden Spanish galleon bound for Spain, he embarked on a treacherous voyage across the Atlantic, braving towering waves that jostled and buffeted the ship. Miraculously, the Archbishop arrived safely in Europe.

Upon reaching the port of Cadiz, Cojico was astonished at the progress achieved by the Europeans. It was remarkable how far humans had evolved from the primitive bipedal creatures he had seen from space thousands of years ago.

"His fellow Izbek had been busy!" He mused, marveling at the panorama of advancements before him. Now, standing on their continent, he could discern their intentions and understand their history simply by clasping his mystical amulet. Once worshipped as gods, they had adapted to the changing world.

Recognizing the enormous wealth gap between the aristocracy and the common people, one fact became clear to thrive in these times, he needed to become a man of influence.

In the ancient city of Monte Alban, Cojico had survived and ruled by assuming the roles of god, emperor and tribal shaman. However, at this moment in time, he figured out that the best path forward lay in the latter guise. Therefore, he set out towards Rome, seeking an audience with the Pope. By the power of persuasion, the holy father granted Cojico's request. He presented his holiness with a jewel-studded solid gold cross known as the Nuestra Senora de Guadalupe, crafted, and fashioned by Juan Diego, after the apparition of the Virgin Mary in Fifteen Thirty One. A priceless treasure from the New World, this relic featured an exquisite, raised engraving of Christ as an infant cradled by his mother.

Impressed by Cojico's devotion to the papacy and captivated by his worldly knowledge, Pope Paul the third appointed him to the esteemed

Curia of Rome, the Papal court, to aid in the governance of the Catholic Church and the Papal States. The Pope gave him a permanent home in Vatican City and a palatial estate in the ancient diocese of Albano, dating back to the fourth century. On this sprawling property, Cojico shed his ecclesiastical robes and human form, allowing his true essence to run free. Transformed into a majestic jaguar, he diligently solved the old villa's rodent problems.

To Cojico, the Church represented an opportunity to keep some semblance of control over humanity.

"If only they knew the truth!" he pondered, aware that the revelation of certain facts, including the origins of humankind, would shatter much of their doctrine.

Utilizing his hypnotic powers to influence the church hierarchy, he ascended to the prestigious College of Cardinals. Using this illustrious position to combat threats to doctrine, specifically from emerging scientific knowledge, the Pope bestowed on him the unofficial title of "defender of the faith." After years of maneuvering himself within the Vatican's social strata, he finally in April Fifteen Eighty Five became Pope Sixtus the Fifth, the last one to use that name.

Under his enlightened leadership, Rome underwent a remarkable transformation. The city shed its drab medieval appearance, blossoming

113

into a vibrant and modern baroque metropolis suffused with grand palaces, sweeping boulevards and resplendent renaissance sculptures that adorned magnificent piazzas. Cojico restructured the church's administrative system, curbing corruption, reorganizing the Secretariat of State, and completely overhauling the Curia's bureaucracy. In this meticulously designed structure, he positioned himself to navigate and shape global events.

During his first reign as Pope, Cojico excommunicated Elizabeth the First of England and Henry the Fourth of France for leading their nations away from Rome's influence towards Protestantism. He feared that this new faith would dismantle feudalism, foster exponential industrialization, and trigger an unprecedented global population explosion.

Reluctantly taking on the mantle of Pope six more times, Cojico amassed an amazing personal fortune. Through the centuries, he assumed various identities, cloaking himself in the shadows to sculpt power behind the scenes. Despite his aversion to the papacy's conspicuous position, he could not resist the allure of Rome.

Today, as Cardinal Roberto Gattuso, he reigns over the Synod of bishops, a position that grants him remarkable sway over the Holy Father, global politics, and environmental affairs.

From his sanctum in Albano, the Cardinal

cherishes the dazzling assemblage of art and antiquities that he has amassed over the years. The walls of his heavily guarded domain display Renaissance masterpieces by Da Vinci, Michelangelo and Titian, alongside more modern works by Van Gogh, Dali, and Picasso. Yet, taking pride of place in the center of his living space, as a reminder of bygone days, sits the splendid Cross of our lady of Guadalupe and the exquisite alebrjes of Cojico, the jaguar sky god of the Zapotec people, skillfully fashioned by the hands of descendants of his former supplicants.

Any would-be cat burglars tempted by envy would do well be to heed the elaborate security systems protecting the Cardinal's treasures. For lurking within these grounds, a colossal feline fiercely prowls, ever watchful and ready to pounce upon intruders with claws of unrelenting fury.

Passage Five.

Present Day Dilemma.

As the centuries flowed by, Cojico moved with the changing times, like a phantom gracefully pirouetting through the delicate dance of life. He shifted and transformed, mimicking death, adopting the visages of his own descendants, ensuring the seamless transfer of his wisdom and wealth across generations.

Sensing that time was of the essence, Cardinal

Gattuso quickly organized a conference call with Sophie Lebole and Zoe Hart two other Izbek castaways and allies. They needed to discuss intelligence provided by the Holy Alliance. In Southern California, humans had unearthed an Escape pod thought lost and the technology held within was a danger to the entire planet. Powerful crystals in the wrong hands held enough energy to destroy continents. During the call, Sophie and Zoe closely examined pictures of the sphere, now sitting in a secret laboratory at the Hoover dam.

The sight of the sphere stirred a deep sadness within them. Tears welled up in their eyes as they recognized it as a symbol of a lost friend and served as a poignant reminder of their longing for home and days gone by.

When Sophie questioned the Cardinal about the source of the information, he revealed the existence of a friend at the CIA who regularly provided updates.

"Just an hour ago," he explained, "they reported no progress opening it."

Zoe expressed concern, sensing that other parties coveted the sphere.

"You know humans will eventually figure it out." Her worry clearly showing on her face.

"And if they do, the consequences could be catastrophic."

Sophie acknowledged the danger, emphasizing the immediate need to prevent unworthy individuals from accessing the sphere's contents. She feared the potential repercussions it could have on human evolution and the delicate balance of the world and beyond. However, retrieving the supplies within the sphere was also crucial. Their amulets needed replenishing and the medical nanites would prolong their lifespans, ensuring their continued survival. Moreover, they could send another message home.

The trio agreed that if humanity took hold of the sphere's contents, they would undoubtedly exploit them for personal gain. It was entirely possible that they would reverse engineer the advanced technology and be able potentially to unlock the secrets of interstellar travel before they were able to understand the complexities.

The Izbek were acutely aware of the impulsive nature of humans and worried about the consequences of inexperienced individuals exploring and expanding into the galaxy. The potential disruption to time and space was alarming, leaving gaping holes in the cosmos, reminiscent of strip-mining operations on Earth.

"We need to reach the sphere!" Zoe declared firmly. And they all concurred.

Once the meeting concluded, Cardinal Gattuso informed the Holy Alliance about the grave threat to the Church and took matters into his own hands. He assumed the responsibility of addressing the issue and booked a private charter with Air Alitalia. Eager to fulfill their mission, the Cardinal, Sophie, and Zoe settled in for the twelve hour journey to Las Vegas Nevada.They spent the first few hours of the flight reconnecting with each other, sharing their own incredible stories of survival. Suddenly, although their amulets had long ago lost most of their energy due to the depleted crystalline energy, they started to vibrate, hinting at a faint message.

Zoe could not hold her excitement.

"Do you sense that? Have they come back for us?"

The message was unclear, leaving Sophie to tightly squeeze her mystical necklace and close her eyes, straining her mind to understand its meaning.

"Maybe if we put all three amulets together."

Sophie suggested, hoping that combining their powers would boost their connection.

Upon realizing the need to be closer to the orbiting ship, the Cardinal requested the pilot to ascend to a higher altitude.

As they interlocked their palms over the amulets, the message miraculously became clear. The Izbek had returned, and their rescue was now imminent.

Overwhelmed with joy, they hugged one another and sank back into their seats. They had been waiting for this day for thousands of years and tears of joy and relief streamed down their faces.

However, all three of their expressions also revealed their concern for the Earth's future. They understood the urgency of informing the rescue vessel about the possibility of the sphere falling into unscrupulous hands. Some survivors had turned rogue and if left unchecked, it could have disastrous consequences for the cosmos. Linking their pendants once again, they cleared their minds and concentrated their telepathic abilities, sending a simple message they hoped the orbiting ship would receive. They would strive to be closer than a thousand miles the next time they tried to contact the Izbek.

High above the Atlantic, with no immediate tasks at hand, they relaxed and enjoyed the flight. Invigorated by the wonderful news, they shared one of Sophie's sumptuous wines and indulged in reminiscing about olden times.

"At least travel times had significantly improved over the years." Zoe laughed.

The Cardinal could not help but shudder as he recalled his journey from the New World on a Spanish galleon. They all reflected on the hardships of old sailing ships, camel caravans, and the discomfort of riding for hours on end.

They looked forward to being back on Izbeckia in a few months and traversing its liquid-plasma tube highways, instantly transported to their desired destinations by the power of their thoughts.

The rest of the flight promised to be uneventful, and they all tried to get some rest, knowing the arduous task that lay ahead.

Upon their arrival in Nevada, a black Escalade sent by the church awaited them at the airport. The Cardinal, Sophie, and Zoe had never been to Las Vegas before, and it served as a stark reminder of how far humanity had progressed. The ancient Izbek had built great cities like Babylon, Thebes, Athens, and Tenochtitlan, but nothing compared to this spectacle. Towering buildings and magnificent hotels stood tall, illuminated by countless blindingly bright lights in a dazzling array of colors. The city was constantly in motion, never standing still.

Despite being near the bustling city, their accommodations in the cathedral compound provided some semblance of tranquility.

Once settled, Sophie and Zoe watched the Cardinal get to work. The CIA had supplied them with a predator drone, which was conveniently sitting on a restricted runway of the Las Vegas airport - a part of the airport reserved primarily for flights to and from Area fifty-one.

The Cardinal unpacked a sleek, black-oversized briefcase made of incredibly durable plastic. From within, he retrieved a ground control station, a futuristic console with a central viewing screen, a keyboard beneath it and a joystick plus a throttle lever on either side.

Preparing to pilot the drone, he resembled someone ready to play a thrilling video game. However, instead of entertainment, he inputted the control codes with precision. At once, the drone's forward view appeared on the screen. The Cardinal diligently checked the rear view and to the side cameras before expertly guiding the drone down the runway and soaring it into the air.

The goal for now was to capture and send real-time images, while also scouring the surrounding area for any signs of potential adversaries.

Knowing they could not get close to the mystical sphere, the Cardinal, Sophie, and Zoe settled into their role as observers. They would patiently await the movements and intentions of others, using they gathered information to strategize their next move. Adapting had always been their strength. However, they understood that once the action started, swift and agile decisions would be crucial. They decided to visit the dam the next morning. But for now, they focused on watching the activity of the scientists and trying to reestablish contact with the Izbek ship, which they knew was tirelessly searching for them.

In the back of their minds, they pondered whether any other Izbek had received the rescue ship's signal.

"Surely not!" they thought.

"Time certainly had depleted their amulets power centuries ago, leaving them with little hope of hearing the long-awaited message."

Sadness briefly drifted into their minds only to be replaced by euphoria.

They were going home.

STORY EIGHT.

THE WOLF GOD.

Passage One.

The Wolf God.

Above the ancient city of Lycopolis ethereal lights illuminated the night sky during full moons, captivating the inhabitants and inspiring artistic expressions. Amid this enchanting backdrop, the revered deity Wepwawet stood as a transformative figure symbolizing courage and divine power in the form of a fearsome wolf.

Known as the "opener of ways," Wepwawet descended to earth in a fiery chariot, commanding respect, and awe among the people of Egypt. As a scout, warrior, and overseer of armies, he played a pivotal role in times of conflict. His followers offered fervent prayers seeking his guidance, aid in battle, and righteous judgment for fallen warriors in the afterlife.

From the moment he arrived on this planet, Wepwawet embraced many guises and assumed countless names. In ancient Egypt, he cunningly masqueraded as the illustrious son of Ra, leading the Pharaoh's armies to victory over the Hyksos and vanquishing the formidable Hittites in the harrowing battle of Kaddish. He traversed the Middle East with a relentless spirit, courageously fighting alongside Saladin during the tumultuous times of the great Crusades.

Passage Two.

Battle of Hattin.

The rhythmic scraping of pumice against the exquisite teardrop pattern Scimitar filled the air. A gentle breeze carried with it the scent of distant thunder, a foreboding hint of the imminent clash of warriors and the inevitable ballet of bloodshed. As he gazed down at his bandaged arm, each fold of cloth whispered tales of past encounters with the relentless Templar Knights and their crimson-cross banners, igniting a fire within Wepwawet's eyes that burned with an unyielding thirst for vengeance.

These Christian warriors had savagely attacked

a Muslim caravan, shedding innocent blood and subjecting survivors to unspeakable horrors. The anguished screams of the women and children still echoed on the desert wind, the acrid stench of carnage carried high into the desert sky, a chilling invitation to the circling vultures. The grave injustice committed by these fanatics had stirred Saladin, the wise ruler of Damascus, to don his armor and wield his sword in defiance. Aware of the danger these deranged men posed, Saladin had pleaded with the king of Jerusalem to bring them to justice. However, his pleas fell upon deaf ears, plunging the region into war.

Determined to strike before Saladin could gather his forces, the Crusaders, under the leadership of the reckless Raynald de Chatillon, embarked on a perilous journey through the blistering desert. They raised the cross that bore the weight of Jesus Christ's suffering. However, trailing the scorching July landscape without sufficient water was sheer folly.

Squinting through stinging eyes, the intense sun and the shimmering waves of heat rising from the sandy furnace conjured mirages of elusive oases. The burdened horses, driven to the brink of madness from thirst, snorted angrily and gnashed their bits, their desperation painfully clear.

Saladin decided against engaging the Crusaders at once, recognizing the benefits of patience and careful planning. This time, he would wait for the Templar knights to come to him, using the advantage of surprise and his knowledge of the local terrain.

Within Saladin's ranks stood an array of skilled and seasoned warriors, none more accomplished or decorated than Wepwawet, now known as Ismael Ulf. As an expert scout, Ismael had a transformative ability to move silently on all fours, slipping through the enemy camp under the cover of darkness like a phantom. Even if the enemy's horses detected Ismael's presence as a prowling wolf, they would lose his trail as he swiftly vanished into the vast expanse of the desert.

Despite his role as the Sultan's second-in-command and architect of the battle strategies, Ismael insisted on leading the fight. Over the years, he had earned a fearsome reputation as a wise and audacious warrior, surviving countless conflicts through his wit and unwavering courage. Commanding a select group of lethal mercenaries, Ismael and his forces moved like shadows, their every motion silent and sure. Each Saracen carried a deadly arsenal, wielding razor-sharp scimitars and curved daggers forged from Damascus folded steel. Their obsidian black handles shaped like African wolves, the Wepwawet emblem, symbolized strength, and cunningness. Lupine motifs adorned their bows and quivers while their arrows carried a lethal poison.

Clad entirely in black, Ismael and his elite assassins blended seamlessly into the night like shadows. Moreover, they forsook helmets and armor, recognizing that speed and agility were their greatest assets.

Ismael's formidable army tightly encircled the trapped Crusaders, with the nearest Christian stronghold miles away and the crucial water source a tortuous six miles behind them.

Unyielding in their arrogance and overconfidence, the Crusaders unknowingly played into Ismael's hands. He envisioned a decisive battle beneath the twin peaks, the horns of Hattin, where Jesus Christ once delivered his sermon.

"Praying to their proclaimed true god wouldn't save them now." Ismael mused.

Despite their desperate need for water, the Crusaders foolishly chose to halt for the night. Seizing this opportunity, Ismael commanded his elite forces to torment them, turning the surrounding hills into a blazing inferno. The knights awoke to a smokey Armageddon, their bodies exhausted from lack of sleep and their throats burning with thirst.

Enveloped in the thick smoke, the Templars stumbled mindlessly, like ants from a disturbed nest, unaware of their enemy's positions. Confusion and anguish gripped a handful of valiant Crusaders as they embarked on a desperate charge, breaking through the Saracen lines and escaping. While Ismael acknowledged their small victory, he knew that the main body of his enemy's army had lost its unity.

Ismael's soldiers unleashed a merciless hail of arrows upon the remaining knights, burdened by their heavy chain mail and forced to fight on foot. Blinded by the swirling sands, the Crusaders struggled to find their footing. An assault on their senses, the acrid smell of sweat mingled with the stench of death and fear. Amidst the chaos, Ismael's loyal dog soldiers fought savagely, their scimitars flashing like lightning bolts. They mercilessly tore through the ranks of the once-proud crusader army with predatory grace, reducing the mighty Templars to a bitter and humiliating defeat.

In a solemn act of loyalty, Ismael personally presented Raynald of Chatillon to Saladin, who judged him for his past atrocities and had him executed, leaving his lifeless body for the vultures to pick clean.

As a testament to their victory, the Saracens triumphantly claimed possession of the sacred relic of the true cross, sending it to Damascus. The defeat of the Christian army opened the door to recapturing Jerusalem and Saladin, accompanied by Ismael Ulf, led his troops towards the holy city.

Passage Three.

Descendant from the Heavens.

Rising boldly from the scorching desert sand, mesas shaped by centuries of wind and weather stood tall and proud. Rocky layers, folded and rolled like ancient scrolls, bore silent witness to the spherical silver craft plummeting from the heavens. It skidded to a dramatic halt, leaving behind a swirling cloud of dust and a ripple in the sand. Wepwawet appeared from the wreckage into the unforgiving heat and blinding sunlight. This barren and arid land stood in stark contrast to his aquatic home on Izbekia, where rivers flowed freely, nourishing vast lakes and oceans. To navigate this unfamiliar territory, Wepwawet's powers of transformation would be tested to their limits.

A few hundred yards from his crash site, Wepwawet spotted a cave in the rust-colored cliffs of a towering mesa. Instinctively understanding the need for shade, he hurried towards the sanctuary of the rocky shelter.

Upon stepping into the cave, he found the ground made of a mosaic of stones. The walls etched with captivating images, whispered of a forgotten era. Vibrant portrayals of creatures roaming a once-verdant landscape mirrored a time long past before the endless tides of sand swallowed this region. Quadrupedal beings frolicked in lush green grasslands, while clear rivers teemed with life. He wondered what manner of creature had left behind this primitive art as a testament to their existence.

As the night took hold and the scorching sun relinquished its grip, the temperature dropped, casting an icy chill. With the magic of his amulet, Wepwawet coaxed warmth from the cave walls, creating a flickering amber glow. As dusk gave way to an ethereal silver moon, stirrings of life appeared from hidden places. Centipedes, scorpions, and spiders scurried about in search of food, while furry creatures pensively looked around, frightened by haunting howls echoing through the cave. Golden wolves, like spectral dancers, weaved in and out of the moonlight, captivating Wepwawet's gaze. Clutching his magical amulet tight, he transformed into a wolf, forging an intimate bond with the essence of this land.

Understanding the gravity of his situation, Wepwawet knew he had to look for a less harsh corner of this unforgiving planet. Grasping his amulet, he realized that many of his fellow castaways had found havens more suited for survival. Though the journey to reach them would be arduous, he knew that reuniting with his former shipmates was imperative if he hoped to find even a semblance of comfort while awaiting rescue.

Moving under the night's cover, taking the form of a wolf, he pressed onward to a fertile valley where a majestic river carved its path towards the ocean. Here, many of his companions had already made considerable progress, securing places where they could thrive. They had assumed the forms of bipedal creatures, resembling their own, yet lacking the intricate intellect and capabilities the Izbek possessed. They had also donned the guises of various beasts. Some called the river their home, others soared through the skies, and a few slithered on the ground, hunting their prey. In their superior wisdom, these extraordinary beings could choose to emulate any living creature, granting them an undeniable advantage over the inhabitants of this newfound world. Their supremacy assured; their domination unquestionable.

During their voyage from Izbekia, their home world, Wepwawet had little interaction with Sobek. However, upon arriving on Earth, an innate connection formed between the two castaways. Sobek took on the form of a mighty crocodile, reigning supreme over the rivers, while Wepwawet assumed the role of a wolf, ruling over the night.

As time unfolded, an unbreakable alliance began to take shape. Along the banks of the Nile, they forged a magnificent civilization. Mortals worshipped them as gods, bestowing reverence upon them for a fleeting moment. United by an unwavering bond, they traversed through the annals of history together, inseparable in their pursuit to assert dominance over the planet. Harnessing the power of humans to further their agendas, they also bestowed upon them intellectual and technological advancements that propelled humanity towards enlightenment.

Their mutual apathy towards the repercussions of manipulating human society only served to fortify the partnership between Wepwawet and Sobek. Yet, the alliance was about to face a grave challenge.

Bold shapeshifters, descendants of the stranded Izbek threatened to shatter the bond between Wepwawet and Sobek and reveal their true identities to the rest of humanity.

Passage Four.

The Assasin.

Centuries had passed since he left the Fertile Crescent, where his escape pod had landed and wandered through Asia Minor, Eastern and Western Europe, weaving amongst the shadows as a lethal assassin for hire.

In the wake of global power shifting westward, most of his fellow Izbek summarily followed, migrating away from the lands where their grand temples once soared.

Wherever they went, they left behind the legacy of half-human, half-animal legends. Those indomitable folktales of were-wolves and other nocturnal beasts haunting the depths of the darkest of terrains, stalking and feasting on unsuspecting souls, will never be forgotten by the peoples that dwelled nearby.

Under the alias of Ulf Cadman, this evil being now lives in the bustling metropolis of New York City. United with Sobek his fellow castaway now known as Martin Krugler, he rekindled a partnership not as gods of antiquity but as titans of industry.

As a skilled negotiator and economic strategist, Ulf is a crucial facilitator for the voracious Sobek corporation. Whenever obstinate foreign governments dared to withhold their treasures, Sobek would dispatch him to bend their wills. He ruthlessly acquired the oil, minerals, and precious metals, with the Sobek corporation only paying a meager stipend for the mining rights.

Martin Krugler also tasked Ulf with the responsibility of orchestrating the evolution of humankind, ensuring that the ancient Izbek clandestinely kept their anonymity while eradicating any threats posed by descendant shapeshifters.

To achieve this goal, Ulf wields absolute control over the dissemination of information, commanding an extensive media empire that stretches across newspapers, television, and the vast realm of social media. Planted strategically in the corners of the globe, his influencers fabricate narratives that serve only the interests of his ilk, quelling any remnants of truth that dare challenge their supremacy. When stories of supernatural beings' bubble to the surface, Ulf distills them into a vat of superstitious hogwash, reduced to mere fairy tales and feeble folklore.

However, despite his omnipotent reach, there come once in a generation instances where Ulf must personally intervene to eradicate a threat. Thus, on this freezing winter's day, he found himself in the desolate wool manufacturing town of Huddersfield West Yorkshire. It was a bitter-cold place, its daunting mill chimneys poised like satanic sentries against a backdrop of somber gray, the air thick with fog that stank of soot.

That night, an extraordinary event was about to unfold on the winter solstice. A young cat changeling was about to appear for the very first time. An extremely rare shapeshifter with the extraordinary ability to peer into the future, capable of unraveling the true intentions of the ancient Izbek, endangering their dominion here on earth.

Ulf Cadman, the Wepwawet wolf, intended to kill Miles Cawtheray.

However, he had underestimated this child's protective mother, who had discovered Ulf lying in ambush.

A voracious wolf attacking a female puma protecting her cub had played out many times before in wilderness areas around the world, but never in the frigid coal cellar of a small mill-terrace house and never with such ferocity.

Flinging each other violently into the walls, the combatants created a tornado of black dust fueled by slashing claws, and snarling jaws. The cacophony of growls and caterwauls from the wolf and the wild cat resonated loudly around that dark-claustrophobic room. The whirling ball of fury spilled into the garden and along a once quiet lane to a wooded thicket. Battered, bruised and bleeding heavily, both animals were limping and close to exhaustion.

Summoning extra strength, Ulf finally managed to throw the cat violently against a tree. As it lay unconscious, he followed up with a crunching death-bite to its head, Ulf killed Edith, Miles's courageous mother. He dumped her carcass onto Bradford Road, a main thoroughfare where many pets had perished under the wheels of passing cars and busses.

However, Ulf did not leave the battle unscathed. Edith had left her mark. His nose and cheek had deep scratches caused by her claws. He had lost part of his right ear. Staring down at his wounds and the puddles of blood, turned solid by the freezing Yorkshire air, he lamented that the problem of Miles Cawtheray would have to wait another day.

STORY NINE.

THE ENCANTADO DOLPHIN.

Passage One.

A Magical Gift.

Julia and Roberto had been struggling to conceive a baby. Roberto spent his days fishing in the Amazon, while Julia sewed vibrant and colorful dresses to sell at the local market. Despite making just enough to make ends meet, they could not afford their own home. They lived in a modest house owned by Julia's family. Every night, in a shared prayer, they yearned for a miracle that would bless them with a child.

In the past few nights, Roberto had experienced vivid dreams while sleeping. In these dreams, a captivating and alluring women appeared from the depths of the river, dancing her way into his bed. Accompanied by soft singing and ethereal music, the woman cast an enchanting spell over Roberto, whisking him away to a secluded glade by the river where she seduced him.

This encounter continued night after night until eventually a full moon illuminated the darkness. After leaving Roberto's dreams, she floated into the mind of his wife, and as Julia tossed and turned, the dream goddess revealed the precious secret that she had bestowed on her. Uncontrollable joy jolted Julia awake, and tears of happiness streamed down her face.

Remembering the stories passed down from her ancestors about the spellbinding river goddess, who would transform into a dolphin to help couples conceive, she decided not to speak of her dreams. Julia did not want to risk losing her precious gift or jeopardize her fisherman husband's livelihood by angering Encantado, who held the power to control the flow of the river, the weather, and the ebb and flow of their lives.

Passage Two.

The Hidden Grotto.

Swept in from the ocean, a heavy icy mist shrouded the entire coast, obscuring the path along the edge of the cliff. This stretch of the Pacific Coast, where the headland intersects with the cold California current, was notorious for its frequent fog. Ill-prepared, the quartet of explorers, Billy, and Robert Carlson, along with their friends Julie and Eric Mears, found their lightweight cotton clothing inadequate against the biting chill. Just that morning, the sun had shone warmly on the red roofs of their homes in Dana Point, but the mist had swiftly rolled in, shrouding everything in its ghostly embrace.

The year was nineteen fifty eight and these young adventurers, fueled by their love for the novels of Nancy Drew and the Hardy boys, sought summer excitement. Dreaming of hidden treasures, they embarked on their quest armed with licorice, potato chips and Coca Cola, crammed into their back packs after a visit to the local grocery store. However, as they labored up the steep slope leading to the grand abandoned mansion on top of the promontory, the weather suddenly turned foul, leaving the kids cold and drenched.

Julie, feeling the chill bite into her bones, voiced her desire to go home.

Billy, the eldest of the group, weighed their options. "It's too dangerous to start down in this weather." He explained. "We can barely see a thing and the last thing we need is to get lost or fall off the cliff."

"Okay, but if we stay here, we'll freeze!" Julie countered, stating the obvious.

"Let's seek shelter in the mansion," Robert bravely suggested.

The old house, erected by the Los Angeles oil mogul, Harvey Wallace, commanded a regal position overlooking the waves as they rolled ashore. It stood upon the spot where the locals and mission monks once passed goods down the treacherous cliff to waiting clipper ships nestled in the bay. On clear days, the mansion offered a breathtaking view of the Pacific Ocean, extending all the way to Catalina Island.

Mr Wallace had spared no expense in creating a luxurious getaway, complete with tennis courts, a swimming pool, and a sinuous stairway leading down to a rugged yet secluded beach. In its heyday, the grand ballroom had played host to lavish parties where imported champagne flowed and guests reveled in sumptuous feasts, dancing the night away to the melodies of a fabulous orchestra. But that was the roaring twenties and a distant memory.

Since the Wallaces lost everything in the great crash of nineteen twenty nine, the house had fallen silent and into disrepair. Unable to sell it or maintain it, the once majestic retreat had transformed into a dilapidated, foreboding structure, now partially veiled by the thick fog enveloping its walls.

Undeterred by the rotting facade, the children entered through the broken door, which emitted a loud spine-tingling creak and added to their trepidation. Inside they found darkness, accompanied by the dank-musty scent of decayed wood. Robert having remembered his flashlight, illuminated a narrow beam that danced against the walls.

People had stripped the interior of the house bare. The iron railings of the sweeping staircase, requisitioned for the war effort, had vanished. Anything of value or reminders of the old house's former grandeur was lost to time. They would have to wait for the fog to burn off, as it often did in the early afternoon, before making their descent down the hill, back to the warmth of their homes. Setting their back packs down, they feasted on candy and fizzy soda pop, seeking comfort in these simple pleasures.

Ever curious, Eric, channeling the spirit of his heroes, the Hardy boys, began to open doors, seeking hidden treasure in unlikely places. Each door revealed the same musty smell and nothing of interest. However, Eric was not giving up. Beyond the remnants of a library, noticeable due to the shelves lining the walls, strewn with tattered pages, he discovered a small trap door measuring three feet square. Made of a solid block of wood, it boasted an ornate lock.

With his trusty pocketknife in hand, Eric managed to pry loose the rust and decay, causing it to finally give way. As the door creaked open, a pungent odor of rotting fish stung their senses. Though the entrance was small, there was sufficient space for a person to enter. A steep and narrow corridor awaited them, directing their descent to a mesmerizing glow of bluish-green light.

Excitedly, Eric jumped inside the corridor and beckoned his friends to join him. "Guys! come on! Let's check this out!" He urged his voice echoing down the passageway.

Eagerly, they squeezed through the door and descended towards the light. The corridor led them into a cavern, where a pool of water shimmered, reflecting light that streamed from an opening in the roof. The stone surfaces of the grotto, weathered smooth by time, displayed pictorial stories from top to bottom. Ancient sailing ships, intricate oceanic maps, and dolphin-deity figurines dancing amidst crashing waves adorned the walls. Next to the pool and off to the side lay a hemp sack tied with simple string.

Robert grabbed it and it felt heavy.

"Somebody's head could be in there." Billy jested, laughing loudly.

"Don't be ridiculous." Robert countered, hesitant to open it and to unveil the mystery.

"I'll do it," Eric said, seizing the opportunity and the package from his friend. Slowly unraveling the string, the sack revealed a dolphin-shaped helmet, engraved with ornate markings reminiscent of Egyptian hieroglyphics and classical Roman dolphin motifs. A haloed light surrounded this mysterious headpiece, captivating the children's gaze.

Encouraged by his friends, Eric could not resist the temptation to try it on. Eagerly, he squeezed his head into the helmet. Instantly, his face became blank, and his eyes blinked with an erratic intensity, resembling the shutters of a naval ship's signaling light. Something unsettling was happening to their friend and fear was visible on their faces.

"Eric, Eric!" They screamed frantically, struggling to remove the helmet. However, Eric remained silent, his face devoid expression. Distraught and afraid, his sister Julie started to cry.

"He'll be fine!" Billy insisted, shaking his friend vigorously by the shoulders. "He's done silly things before."

Although Julie remained unconvinced, it took several agonizing minutes before they were finally able to snap Eric out of his trance.

"What the heck happened?" Robert questioned, studying Eric, whose once-flushed face had now turned ghostly white.

Seated close to the pool, trembling with a mix of fear and fascination, Eric recounted his experience. The helmet had tightened its grip on his skull, projecting an incredibly vivid dream into his mind. He told a story of a ship pushed onto the treacherous rocks below the point, by a violent winter storm. A sailor, magically and godlike transformed into a dolphin. Braving the tempestuous elements and by calming the waters, he appeased the thunder, wind, and rain, and rescued each crew member. The dolphin carried them away from the perilous rocks towards the gentle shoreline of Capo beach.

The cave fell silent, with only the whispers of a breeze. Suddenly, without warning, a distressed and agitated dolphin erupted from the surface of the pool, its screeches echoing around the cavern. Horrified, the children recoiled, their screams rebounding from the stone walls.

Overwhelmed and bewildered, Eric accidentally dropped the helmet into the water, watching as it quickly sank.

Terrified, they sprinted out of the cave, scrambling up the steep passageway, all the while the disgruntled dolphin continued to voice its displeasure.

"What about the helmet?" Eric questioned, reluctant to leave it behind.

"Are you suggesting we go back down there?" Julie retorted. "No way!" She exclaimed, mirroring the sentiments of her fellow adventurers. No one desired to confront that angry dolphin.

Struggling with the house's stubborn door, they exited to find that the fog had completely cleared. Descending the cliff and returning home with renewed courage, they vowed to revisit the enchanting blue-green grotto.

Unfortunately, the following week a demolition crew deprived them of their adventure by flattening the old mansion. In its place, they built a hotel, restaurant, and retirement community, providing others with the same breathtaking view over the Pacific Ocean.

Passage Three.

Dancing through the Waves.

According to her grandmother, Sarah Sirent's family traced their ancestry back to the small settlement of Fort of São José do Rio Negro in Brazil, which later became Manaus, the largest city in the Amazon basin. From the day she was born, her grandmother told Sarah that she was special, descended from the indigenous Manaós peoples who eked out a living by working the land in search of precious metals and fishing the great river. In eighteen forty eight, upon hearing the news of the gold discovery at Sutter's Mill in the Sierra Nevada foothills of California, her great-great-grandfather hopped a Portuguese trading ship bound for San Francisco. The story, though blurred, tells of a shipwreck off the coast before he could make it to the gold fields. Although he did not make a fortune, he was able to buy a small fishing boat, married a local girl, and settled along the same coast that had claimed the ship that had carried him to America.

Sarah has an angelic voice that engagingly finds release within the sanctuary of her shower. The cascade of water flowing over her body sparks an irresistible urge to sing. As though water is a seductive muse that exerts a magnetic pull on her, just like nectar draws honeybees to flowers.

It was on her thirteenth birthday, beneath the ethereal illumination of a full moon, that Sarah finally unraveled the origin of her connection with water. It comforts her like nothing else, and this realization unveils a remarkable love affair with the aquatic realm that extends far beyond the confines of her bathroom.

On weekends, Sarah rides her bicycle to the expansive Pacific Ocean near her home, passing by immaculate white boats anchored along the wharf in Dana Point. One vessel, The Pilgrim, a nineteenth-century clipper ship, commands her attention as she makes her way to the harbor wall. There, she securely fastens her bicycle to a viewing bench using a bright red chain and combination lock, ensuring its safety in her absence.

From there, Sarah skips down a few stairs onto the sandy beach and ventures past a towering headland, searching for privacy in a secluded cove hidden from prying eyes. Taking a deep breath, she spreads her beach towel, secures her belongings within her satchel, and savors the faint tang of salt carried by the fresh ocean breeze.

Her excitement rising, fueled by a thrilling anticipation, Sarah brims with vitality and eagerness to embark upon yet another aquatic adventure. A perfect California morning greets her, with the sun poised to climb into a cloudless, blue sky. Gulls resembling tiny kites dance overhead near her cliffside home. Sarah briefly wonders if her father was appreciating the day's beauty or consumed by work in his basement.

As Sarah races towards the water's edge, she avoids tripping on the scattered rocks dotting the shoreline. Today is meant for relishing life, not surrendering to the shackles of a job. As she enters the ocean, the invigorating chill of the surf envelops her body, causing a miraculous transformation. She morphs from an impish, slender-legged adolescent imbued with playfulness into a sleek, silver-shiny dolphin, leaping gracefully out of the water, twirling in mid-air, and propelling herself past the headland. Sarah revels in the ocean's depths, embracing the waves wrapping around her body. Her playful pirouettes mesmerize local fishermen on half-day charters, invoking radiant smiles as she engages them in chattering conversation.

Amidst the spray, Sarah's thoughts resonate. "If only people understood," she muses.

"They would follow me around the backside of Catalina Island, to where the seafloor plunges into the abyss, revealing a bountiful trove teeming with colossal yellowfin tuna, vibrant red snapper, and elusive striped bass." Alas, humans for all their enlightenment, have yet to discover the ability to talk with the animals.

During her aquatic escapades, Sarah indulges in a few mackerels, a delectable snack rejuvenating her energy before bidding farewell to the sea. With the ability befitting a world-class long boarder, she skillfully rides the rhythmic swells and colossal breakers, expertly navigating her way back to shore.

As darkness blankets the coastline, Sarah returns to the familiar sanctuary of the cove, swiftly collecting her belongings and retrieving her bicycle from the wharf. She hurries home before her parents have time to grow concerned.

Sarah's unwavering love for the water, her undeniable affinity for the deep blue, continues to weave its mesmerizing spell, promising a future full of adventures that will carry her to even greater depths within the transcendental ocean.

STORY TEN.

THE APE.

Passage One.

West African Prophecy.

I n the tapestry of West African mythology, the figure of Kuri stands as a captivating enigma. Born from the celestial union of the sky and the earth, Kuri defies convention by descending to the earthly realm as a shooting star and choosing to walk among the Hausa tribe in Nigeria rather than remain aloof in the heavens like his own kind. This intimate connection with mortals weaves a rich cultural fabric, where Kuri embodies the intricate balance between light and shadow, benevolence and cunning, harmony, and discord.

With a masterful command of transformation, Kuri embodies a duality that transcends mere mortal understanding. He seamlessly transitions between the form of a captivating young man bedecked in resplendent attire and ethereal purple jewelry, to that of a mischievous baboon whose barks echo through the wilderness, embodying the primal forces of the natural world. Legends whisper of Kuri's ability to embody the very elements themselves, wielding lightning and fire with a capricious whim that blurs the boundaries between the known and unknown.

As Kuri descended from the celestial expanse, a cacophony of voices welcomed the enigmatic being to the realm of Oyo, a vibrant kingdom nestled amidst the verdant forests and rolling hills of West Africa. Kuri's presence mesmerized the people of Oyo, their eyes wide with wonder at this ethereal entity that had graced their land.

Kuri's voice resonated, captivating the villagers with its melodic timbre. He told of a time when powerful tribes from distant lands would come to steal their children and take their ancestral home.

Passage Two.

The Rumbler.

Yet, Kuri's whimsical nature and penchant for

chaos often set him at odds with his celestial kin, challenging the order of the heavens with his unpredictable ways. Kuri's offspring inherited fragments of his essence, each a reflection of his enigmatic spirit. Among them, Gurum-Gurum stands out as the "rumbler," a colossal ape shapeshifter whose thunderous fury manifests in earthquakes that shake the very foundation of human arrogance, demanding reverence for the divine in all its forms.

Passage Three.

Dambe.

Nestled high on the Jos Plateau in the heart of Berom tribes' ancestral lands lay the village of Gwol. Here, amidst the beautiful scenery and undulating terrain, adobe huts fabricated from dried mud bricks sat on level ground beneath the granite rock formations atop a hillside adorned with a forest-grassland mosaic. These primitive cylindrical dwellings, topped with thatched grass roofs, ensured that the interior stayed dry during the wet season. The architectural construction offered relief from the summer heat, while in the winter months, fires blazed within the huts, radiating warmth rebounding from the clay walls. These dwellings, resembling cones protruding from the earth, surrounded a more elaborate home at the center of the settlement like termite hills spreading out from an original colony.

Within this community, a young man named Davou blossomed. Born to humble parents who tended the land and hunted, he had the spirit and strength of a lion. Despite being only sixteen, he boasted the chiseled physique of any famed gladiator. When wrestling or boxing, he outshined not only the boys but fully grown men in his village and the surrounding countryside. The call of adventure beckoned him. A chance to prove his worth beyond these hills, to embrace the unknown.

As the rainy season approached, a chance for change dangled before him in the form of a journey to Kano. Northern traders recognized Davou's formidable talent in hand-to-hand combat. They offered his family a fortune to apprentice him as a Dambe fighter and to become skilled in that intricate martial art in the grand city. Reluctant at first, his father eventually agreed, knowing this opportunity could lift his family out of poverty.

Although hesitant to leave the only home he had ever known, Davou's excitement bubbled within him. The prospect of leaving the clay dirt behind and setting off on an adventure filled his heart with anticipation. Accompanied by his eldest brother, they embarked on their journey towards Kano, a majestic city built at the confluence of two waterways to form the Hadeija River that would flow eastwards towards Lake Chad.

The first thing that Davou noticed was the oppressive heat once they descended the escarpment from the plateau, leaving behind the milder climate. The city stood proudly surrounded by a majestic encircling wall, and its ornately decorated buildings evoked visions of emperors and royalty. The magnificent mosque with its twin minarets seemed to touch the heavens, stirring amazement within Davou's very soul.

As he weaved through the bustling streets, the diverse array of people from everywhere left him mesmerized. The scent of exotic spices and incense mingled in the air, intoxicating his senses. The southern terminal of the Trans-Sahara trade route had brought together a tapestry of cultures. Languages, sounds, colors, and smells intermingled harmoniously. In the heart of the city, the emir's palace and central square were a testament to Tubali style architecture. The walls, archways, and facades, ornately exteriorized with patterns and vibrant colored textures, shone in the sunlight as testaments to the skilled artisans that perfected this craft.

Kano's Great Mosque adorned with stark white plaster shimmered in the heat haze rising, encouraged by the burning sunlight, and stood as a testament to the city's grandeur. Within its walls, the twin minarets from which calls fell upon the devout ushering them to prayer seemed to stretch towards the heavens. This magnificent structure, housing the sacred scriptures brought back from Mecca, seemed to him to defy gravity. Gold inlays gracefully adorned both the inside and outside walls. The temple stood in stark contrast to his own beliefs and upbringing. His grandfather raised him to show reverence to Dagwi, the father of the sun.

Listening to the imams, he pondered what his spiritual journey ahead might entail. As Davou settled into his new life, his unparalleled talent as a fighter propelled him towards his destiny. Serving his apprenticeship as a Dambe fighter, he found himself enslaved, forced into martial arts contests organized by rival traders and merchants who kept a stable of gladiators. Fortunes ebbed and flowed with the outcomes of these contests, where Davou's skills promised his handlers victory and success.

Dambe, considered unseemly by the aristocracy and elite, was strictly a sport for the lower caste groups. However, they recognized its importance as a training ground for combat, with many techniques and terminologies drawing parallels to warfare. The aristocracy's interests lay in horses and the annual Durban equestrian festival. While this celebration primarily highlighted skilled equestrians, musicians and circus performers also took the stage. The city bustled with people as merchants promoted fights, enticing spectators to wager on the outcomes.

Through his victories, Davou gained a reputation as a skilled fighter, making it increasingly challenging for his merchant handlers to find him worthy opponents. As the Durban festival approached, it seemed unlikely he would have a challenger. Yet, fate intervened as the city swelled with visitors to see the colorful spectacle of rival families' horses and unparalleled equestrian skills.

A notorious slave trader named Gurum, known for his thirst for combat, came forward as Davou's only opponent, wagering heavily on himself to win. In the bustling market square, a showdown unlike any other awaited as the two fighters entered the makeshift battlefield. The air buzzed with anticipation as Davou, the undefeated slave fighter, faced Gurum, the freeman fighting for pleasure, his confidence radiating from a mysterious purple talisman around his neck.

As the traditional percussive music filled the air driving the crowd into a rhythmic frenzy, the fighters' handlers readied them to engage in a dance of strength and skill. They wrapped Davou's fists tight, ready to strike with power, while Gurum exuded a supernatural strength. The crowd erupted as the fierce battle began, with both men vying for victory.

In intense three-round matches with no time limits, the fighters displayed their skill and determination, their bodies glistening with sweat as they exchanged powerful blows. Davou, facing a formidable opponent in Gurum, found himself in a contest for the ages, the spectators electrified by the raw energy unfolding before them.

In a climactic moment, Gurum delivered a devastating blow that sent Davou reeling, leading to his defeat. As Davou lay unconscious, Gurum's victory sealed, his handlers loaded him onto a slave wagon bound for the port city of Onim (Lagos). Destined for sale to Portuguese traders sailing to the Americas. Gurum, the man who had bested him, now led the procession towards his uncertain future.

Awakening in a caged wagon, chained, and surrounded by others in the same plight, Davou realized the harsh reality of his defeat. Sold into servitude by his merchant handlers who could not cover the wager, he knew he would never again roam the rolling hills of his ancestral home on the Jos Plateau, never feel the cool African breeze on his face or hear its whispers of ancient history. Davou's journey had taken an unexpected turn, plunging him into a world of uncertainty and hardships beyond his imagination.

Passage Four.

A World Away.

Enduring the unspeakable horrors of the 'middle passage,' where the ocean's unforgiving waves whispered tales of suffering and despair, Davou landed on American soil, his spirit unbroken, his will unwavering. Gadsden's wharf in Charleston, South Carolina, bore witness to his arrival, a mere steppingstone on the treacherous path to greatness that destiny had laid out for him amidst a landscape colored by injustice and cruelty.

Shackled and in chains, angry men linked Davou to a coffle of downtrodden souls. Davou trudged through the scorching heat of the sun-baked streets, etching his first steps in a foreign land. Looking at the ground, he contemplated his fate, yearning for his home on the Jos Plateau and the cool breeze blowing down from the granite hills. Ahead, women marched barefoot, their resilience echoing in each step they took. Behind them, their overseers, mounted on steeds of privilege, exuded authority with pistols glinting at their hips and whips poised for cruelty. Yet Davou, now known as David, drew strength from the depths of his African heritage, fortitude as unyielding as the roots of an ancient baobab tree.

As the shadows of the American Civil War loomed large, fate offered David a chance at freedom. Seizing the opportunity in the absence of his owner, who had left to join the Confederate cause, David broke the chains of bondage and embarked on a journey westward, seeking solace amidst the vast expanse of the Indian Territory, where the echoes of freedom whispered sweet promises.

In the embrace of the Cherokee, Cree, and Seminole, David found a new home, a sanctuary where his past dissolved into the winds of change, where he learned the language of the land and honed the art of survival. The proclamation of Emancipation ushered in a new chapter, where David Blake rose from the ashes of slavery, a free man destined for greatness.

Returning to South Carolina, David tilled the land with pride, but destiny had grander plans for him. A call to service as a U.S. deputy marshal beckoned, propelling him into the annals of history as the first Black deputy to serve beyond the Mississippi, a pioneer of justice in the untamed lands of the West.

For over three decades, David Blake stood as a stalwart defender of justice, a beacon of hope in a lawless frontier. Clad in the garb of righteousness, he wielded his Winchester rifle and Colt revolver with precision, facing down the most notorious outlaws of his time.

In his twilight years, David's legacy bloomed like a wildflower on the prairie. He nurtured his children under the radiant glow of knowledge and wisdom that he bestowed upon them, ensuring they understood and embraced their heritage rooted in the tumultuous history of Africa and the oppressive chains of servitude.

Retiring in comfort, his heart brimming with tales of valor and survival, David Blake stood as a testament to the indomitable spirit, a phoenix risen from the ashes of adversity, his legacy a testament to the enduring power of determination and resilience, a beacon of inspiration for his family and generations yet to come.

In the fading light of a warm summer evening, David Blake sat on the wooden porch of his modest homestead in South Carolina, a sense of contentment settling over him like a familiar cloak. The whispers of the past lingered in the rustling leaves, carrying tales of endurance and triumph. Memories of the Jos Plateau and the cool breeze from the granite hills flooded his mind, a bittersweet reminder of a distant home.

As he gazed out at the sprawling fields before him, a sense of gratitude washed over him. "Thank you, ancestors, for guiding me through the darkest of nights," he whispered, feeling their presence in the gentle rustle of the wind.

The shadows of the past intertwined with the promise of a brighter future as David reflected on his journey from slavery to freedom, from bondage to justice. "I may have been shackled in body, but my spirit was always free," he mused, his eyes fixed on the setting sun painting the horizon in hues of gold and crimson.

In the stillness of the evening, a sense of peace settled within him, a quiet assurance that his legacy would endure long after he was gone. "My children will carry on the flame of resilience and courage," David vowed, his heart overflowing with pride for the generations yet to come.

As darkness descended, enveloping the world in its embrace, David Blake, the pioneer of justice, the defender of the oppressed, closed his eyes for the final time, the echoes of a life well-lived resounding in his soul. And amidst the symphony of cicadas and the soft rustle of the wind, his spirit soared, a testament to the enduring power of determination and resilience in the face of adversity.

STORY ELEVEN.

THE EAGLE GOD

Passage One.

God in the Heavens.

Nestled below the majestic Coatepec mountain, a tapestry of vibrant traditions unfolds in central Mexico. It is a canvas where echoes of Aztec heritage harmoniously blend with the rhythms of Catholicism, a symphony expressed through the tongues of Spanish, Latin, and the ancient language of Classical Nahuatl.

In this valley, the deities of old, their spirits still vibrant, find support alongside the Madonna. In humble houses and ancient temples, fervent prayers rise like incense, seeking blessings from the ancient gods and Jesus Christ for their families.

The faithful turn their gaze towards the heavens and Huitzilopochtli, an extraterrestrial deity born from the ethereal fusion of hummingbirds and the brave souls of warriors. In the hearts of the Nahuatl, his presence is a beacon of hope and a guardian against malevolence.

Like an eagle, he soars with divine purpose, his wings outstretched against the backdrop of the sky. His presence orchestrates swift justice, sending a tremor through those who nurture evil intentions. Water, coveted and cherished, finds sanctuary beneath his enchanted feathers. These glistening droplets bestow life-giving sustenance to the fertile soil.

Behind him, thunder resonates, casting an invisible shield upon his faithful followers, safeguarding their crops, homes, and loved ones from harm's cruel grasp.

Near Coatepec Mountain, the rhythmic heartbeat of faith harmonizes with the ebb and flow of life, an ode to the timeless traditions that permeate the very fabric of this sacred land.

Passage Two.

The Specter of the City.

If you live in East Los Angeles, where fear pervades the night, you walk quickly from place to place. No dawdling, as that is when trouble finds you. An hour or so ago, Juan Aguirre had finished his shift at the glitzy steakhouse in Beverly Hills. Now, he found himself back in his humble neighborhood along Figueroa Street. This immigrant community, predominantly Mexican but with sprinklings of Hondurans and Guatemalans, held a certain charm. However, the neighborhood had become less safe over the years, gradually succumbing to the influence of San Salvador's notorious street criminals who had infiltrated with their menacing gangs.

His mother had reminisced about better times when the neighborhood flourished with joy. Families strolled the streets without fear, enjoying vibrant eateries and reveling in street fiestas that colored the summer nights. But those days were long gone.

Many local businesses had moved, and the ones that stayed shut their doors early and barricaded behind iron bars.

His mother's voice echoed in his thoughts, lamenting that things had changed.

"We could all go out, eat, and have a good time." She would mournfully say. "But now you can't even step out of your house without the grim reality of never returning home."

Juan quickened his pace from the bus stop, eager to reach his family's safety. As he made his way, he had to pass a scrap metal yard and an old tire recycling facility, guarded by a massive metal gate and fence, adorned with barbed wire.

It baffled him why there was so much security to protect trash. The feeble streetlights offered little comfort in this dimly lit part of the city, further intensifying the eerie atmosphere. Struggling to see inside, Juan found it to be a dark and ominous place at night.

The sole source of color emanated from the faint glow of a desk lamp and the flickering television inside the security guard's shed, nestled just inside the sprawling yard. Shadows danced menacingly on the mounds of junk, conjuring images of mythical monsters and fearsome beasts.

Every night, Juan noticed the guard slumped inside, lost in the hypnotic glow of the television, or engrossed by his phone. He had never seen the guard on his rounds, leading him to believe this job came with a surplus of leisure time.

"A cushy job," he thought sardonically, "for someone who likes to sleep during the day."

However, on this night, an unsettling silence hung in the air as the guard's shed stood empty, save for the faint sound of a sports broadcast emanating from the television set. Juan paid it no mind and continued his walk home. But then, out of the corner of his eye, a massive, charcoal figure swooped down from the sky. He felt a fierce rush of wind and heard a gut-wrenching crack, like a blistering bullwhip.

Startled, Juan strained his eyes to see what had made that sound. Yet, in an instant, the enigmatic entity vanished, leaving a calm stillness within the yard. All he could make out were the towering stacks of black tires and heaps of rusting metal.

With trepidation coursing through his veins, he hurried home.

The following day brought news that left the neighborhood buzzing with chatter. The police had discovered and apprehended four gang members arranged side by side, like iced fish on a market stall, just a stone's throw away from the abandoned guard's shed. The police recovered the contents of a broken safe, two pistols, one revolver, four machetes, and a semi-automatic assault rifle.

Medical personnel found the security guard on the lawn in front of the local emergency room with a cracked skull and knife wound. When questioned, he could not remember how he had arrived at the hospital. Miraculously one week later, and all patched up, the doctors released him. He thanked his god, relieved to have survived the members of Mara Salvatrucha.

Passage Three.

The Eagle.

Jose Aguilar had always longed to defy gravity and soar through the sky like a bird. When sleeping, his imagination whisked him away to a magical realm, where he glided above pyramids, majestic-regal castles, and towering cathedrals. Through his dreamscape, he would navigate across vast forests and gracefully swoop down over cascading waterfalls. Yet, at times, he would venture even higher, soaring above the cotton wool clouds until he reached the pinnacle of the world.

His beloved grandfather, a wellspring of wisdom and love, often regaled him with tales of their noble lineage. Jose's heart cherished these stories, which depicted a proud and powerful race of avian beings interwoven with humanity. The Tengu are fierce warriors who soared in the Japanese skies, the Boobries haunted the craggy northern isles of Scotland, and the Thunderbirds safeguarded the native peoples of North America. Fables and myths about bird people beckoned from every corner of the globe. His grandfather believed with unwavering conviction that these mystical beings continued to exist in America, the land they call home.

Upon the heart-wrenching loss of his parents in a senseless drive-by shooting, Jose moved from East Los Angeles, traveling south to live with his tender-hearted grandfather in San Juan Capistrano. Their humble home nestled on Alipaz Street, bordered the last working farm in the mission town. Going about his daily routine, Jose was fortunate to see rabbits and even coyotes. However, the most frequent visitor was a graceful, red-shouldered hawk.

Jose affectionately named him "Red," and he always seemed to arrive when story time began. He would settle on the eaves of their home, listening to the incredible fables woven by Jose's grandfather as he savored his beer. At the same time, Jose sipped on an orange soda. Red would stay, enchanted by the stories, until it was time to hunt. He would lend a helping hand to the local farmers in their ceaseless struggle against ravenous rodents devouring their crops.

Under the radiant glow of a harvest moon, casting its gossamer-like illumination upon the expansive coastline from Laguna Beach to Oceanside, Jose celebrated his thirteenth birthday.

On this sacred night, he met Red again, soaring above the time-worn mission. Guided at the behest of a feint celestial call, they journeyed inland, their flight tracing the snaking bends of the Ortega highway eastward, ascending above the undulating coastal hills. They swooped down in a swift ballet over the tranquil waters of Lake Elsinore before eventually returning home.

This time, it felt palpably more real than any ephemeral fantasy. Assuming his avian form within the perception of a dream, Jose's wings spread wide, their span dwarfing that of his faithful Red. In his transformed state, he felt endowed with a newfound strength, a sinewy power coursing through his entire body.

Unable to hold his exhilaration, Jose told

his grandfather about the dream, sharing the wondrous spectacle he had seen while soaring in the heavens. In a solemn affirmation, his grandfather assured him that this was not merely a dream. Still, rather, it was a sign of his destiny; a divine calling bestowed upon him by the gods.

"You have been chosen!" his grandfather affirmed; his weathered voice laced with reverence. "This is a sacred gift that others may never understand. Beware, for there will be others like you, and while some are benevolent, others are evil and treacherous. Blessings have graced you and in time, shapeshifting will become as natural as putting on your shoes."

Initially, Jose doubted the validity of his grandfather's words, attributing them to the vagaries of old age. However, his doubts left him during the following lunar solstice. As the moon ascended over the vast Pacific Ocean, Red joined him again, bowing his head in reverence before continuing his lessons.

While the exact nature of his destiny remained shrouded in uncertainty, Jose harbored an unwavering resolve - a longing to exact retribution for the loss of his parents and cleanse their old neighborhood of violence and gangs. He would focus on sculpting a haven where people could walk the streets without fear.

STORY TWELVE.

THE SKIN-WALKER.

Passage One.

The Skin-walker.

"Yee Naaldlooshi," means walks on all fours, a name that instills dread into the hearts of the Navajo people. Within the depths of their cultural folklore, witches take on the guise of men, often appearing as ravens or coyotes. The pinnacle of their power grants them the ability to tap into the raw energy of nature, allowing them to transform seamlessly into any creature.

Possessing unparalleled agility and speed, these elusive beasts prove impossible to capture. With eerie ability, they pry into the depths of one's thoughts, effortlessly imitating voices and ensnaring unsuspecting souls towards their untimely demise. Ensnared by the curses of malevolent and disillusioned people, these witches unfailingly bring misfortune. Their presence yields disfigurement, death, and the indelible scars that they leave on both individuals and entire communities.

The Navajo people interacted with and were both educated and influenced by the many tribes that bordered their lands, including the early Pueblo communities and the Ute nation.

During periods of peace, they would gather in the springtime to trade, where an array of items such as baskets, pelts, clothing, and vibrant turquoise jewelry would exchange hands. The two tribes would sit around the fire and regale each other with tales of courage in battle and exaltations of their masculinity when confronted by the chilling presence of malevolent spirits.

Therefore, it would not be an unfounded notion to surmise that all the native peoples of Nevada, Utah, and those that entered these lands would also revere and fear the enigmatic "skin-walkers."

Passage Two.

Hell on Earth.

The setting sun over the Truckee River paints the sky with all the vibrant colors on a skilled artist's palette. Behind them now was the forty mile desert, a waterless, alkali wasteland, and the most dreaded section of the California Trail. Pioneers traversed it in August, at the height of summer, during the cooler nighttime hours to avoid the blistering heat and the scorching sun.

This specific time of year was crucial for crossing, as travelers aimed to reach the Sierra Nevada Mountains before winter arrived and blocked access through the passes with heavy snow. Just one year prior, the perilous experience of a particular group at the Donner Pass serves as a haunting reminder. With no way to escape, they resorted to cannibalism, consuming the flesh of their companions to stay alive.

"What does human flesh taste like?" Jonas wondered to himself.

"Hey, Jonas, hold up on those mules!" His father instructed, "We will camp over there tonight."

Jolted out of his daydream, Jonas Simon abruptly steered the worn wagon off the trail and towards a small clearing hidden amongst the thick brush, halting next to a stunted, close-coned pine tree and a large clump of sage grass. It was imperative to make camp before the sun disappeared behind the majestic mountains before them and cast its long shadows over their weary bodies. Finally free from the terrible ordeal of traversing the hellish Forty miles, the trio exhaled a collective sigh of relief.

The scorching heat made the mules unruly. Carcasses of their dead cousins littered the trail.

Their bleached bones shone like macabre beacons in the bright moonlight.

The sickening crunch beneath the wagon's wheels only frightened the already skittish animals further, making them ready to bolt.

The treacherous two-day journey through a hell-like wasteland had become a death sentence for many pioneers. Both humans and animals alike had succumbed to the torment of thirst, their bodies drying to a crisp under the unrelenting sun.

Fortunately, Jonas's father was wise beyond measure. He had prepared for such an eventuality. He had saved empty feed barrels and filled them with life-sustaining water from the Humboldt River before it sank into the arid desert.

With relief flooding their hearts, they left the desert behind, ready to face the next daunting challenge, the arduous ascent over the towering mountains that lay ahead.

While Jonas meticulously arranged kindling to make a fire, a curious sight caught his attention. Below the foothills, large Chinese kites breathed life into the air, acrobatically maneuvering in the wind.

"Something's interesting those buzzards," remarked Indian Pete, his father's partner, and fellow prospector. The black-feathered undertakers circled above, and their ominous descent foreshadowed the misfortune awaiting someone below.

An uneasy chill ran down Jonas's spine, but despite

his apprehension, his sense of adventure pushed him to investigate the commotion when they passed that way the next day. Settling by the fire next to his father, who was already fast asleep, Jonas drifted into dreamland as dawn approached. Morning arrived quickly for the weary travelers. Jonas's father tended to the mules, understanding that their well-being was paramount. Their strength and resilience ensured their survival in this unforgiving and never-ending wilderness.

With a sense of responsibility, Jonas gathered the bedrolls and organized the wagon. Indian Pete prepared a hearty breakfast of biscuits, salt-pork, and beans, washed down by steaming strong coffee.

Once his father doused the fire, they set out and began the ascent into the foothills, following the well-defined route previously blazed by those who had ventured south from the Oregon Trail. As Jonas kept his eyes peeled for signs of the previous night's aerial spectacle, something unexpected happened. A solitary vulture took flight, panicked by their arrival.

"Look, Dad!" Exclaimed Jonas, pointing eagerly ahead.

Intrigued and concerned for the welfare of any fellow travelers, he convinced his father that they should investigate. Halting the mules, Jonas's father hoisted him onto the back of his horse, and together they walked toward the clearing. As the morning sun began to bake the earth, a shimmering haze and an eerie stillness enveloped them. They dismounted and cautiously walked forward, Indian Pete trailing closely behind.

Remarkably, in the heart of the clearing was a set of Native American garments, most likely Navajo and those of a gold miner, discarded in the dust. Viewing what they had discovered, Pete thought it strange because they were deep in Ute territory and miles away from Navajo lands.

Alongside the clothing was the well-preserved pelt of a coyote, with strange symbols drawn in the sand. A large red patch, assumed to be blood, seeped into the ground, and a splattering of red drops headed east. They followed the blood for no more than twenty paces. Then it disappeared alongside more symbols etched in the sand, leaving only the sagebrush and a scurrying lizard diving for cover.

Ashen-faced and filled with worry, Indian Pete stood trembling at the edge of the clearing. He refused to venture further, muttering something under his breath that sounded like "skin-walker." Jonas and his father looked all around, but they found no sign of a body or a carcass.

Captivated by the coyote pelt, Jonas was about to reach for it as a keepsake when Pete abruptly rushed in, forcefully yanking him away. In Pete's eyes was a deep seriousness, a conviction that something wicked had passed through here, and he did not want it to join them on their journey.

Taken aback by the sudden tug on his shirt, Jonas

turned to meet Pete's grave stare.

"Leave it be!" Pete commanded; his voice filled with authority. "Only misfortune will follow if we bring that thing along!"

Reluctantly, Jonas stepped away, his shoulders slumped in disappointment. He had genuinely wanted to keep the pelt as a souvenir.

"Best be on our way," his father intervened. "Whatever happened here is beyond our understanding. Strange things happen in the wilderness!"

Indian Pete nodded in solemn agreement, the yearning to leave this place clear in his eyes.

Jonas climbed back aboard the wagon, pointing it west and toward the dream of California gold.

Passage Three.

The Scourge of the Navajo.

Sinauf yearned for home. It had been ten thousand years since his escape pod crash-landed on Earth, following a catastrophic event that left the mother ship in ruins. With scarce resources and limited options, only a select few Izbeks had undertaken the arduous journey back to their distant home —a voyage spanning eons. Sinauf's escape pod careened away from his fellow castaways, hurtling through the clouds until it crashed onto the peak of a huge mountain. It tumbled down the slope and came to a halt at the treeline. Concealing his pod in a cave obscured by dense conifers, Sinauf beheld a stunning panorama of white-capped granite teeth and lush green valleys.

Within this bountiful landscape lived a tribe of paleo-humans, their territory teeming with life, traversed by crystal-blue rivers and streams. In this wondrous landscape, an array of majestic creatures thrived: ancient bison, wild antelope, and camelops roamed freely, while large-toothed tigers and dire wolves stealthily pursued their prey, reveling in the abundance of this unspoiled habitat. Grateful for his stroke of fortune, Sinauf discovered that this land provided him with everything necessary for survival. Assuming the guise of a human, he only interacted and immersed himself in the everyday life of these primitive people when necessary.

Using his immense powers, Sinauf deployed his wisdom and the dedicated labor of these people to forge a more prosperous civilization. He built a cavernous retreat below a protective ridge, nestled between a pair of buttes that resembled the ears of a bear. From here, he looked down over the valley to the south, now revered by the primitive people as a place where a god holds sway—an awe-inspiring testament to their devotion. As Sinauf eagerly awaited rescue and the return of the Izbeks, he withdrew into a secluded life within the temple-cave, becoming a revered holy man and God. He ventured into the valley incognito, assuming the form of a wolf or coyote when seeking sustenance.

However, from his lofty perch, he saw the ebb and flow of countless generations, their lives as transient as raindrops falling from the sky. Seeking a way to contact his home planet, Sinauf could not sit idly by and wait for rescue. He traveled on many occasions to visit other majestic mountains even higher than the one he called home. In these icy realms, he searched for a cache of powerful crystals left behind by their mother ship to cultivate, but with no success.

Hence, in fifteen forty, Sinauf, the marooned Izbek now named Tyrone Sani, joined an expedition led by the infamous Francisco Vasquez de Coronado. Tyrone was excited to search for gold and hoped to find treasures that rivaled the fantastic Aztec riches discovered by the Spanish in Mexico, as well as the ethereal power crystals planted by his fellow crew members.

Apart from Tyrone, this expedition was not without its colorful characters. An adventurous scoundrel and local guide, El Turco (or the Turk), had convinced Coronado that he held the secrets to seven wondrous cities dripping with gold.

With eager anticipation, the expedition marched north into the Rio Grande Valley, only to discover humble and primitive townships of Pueblo indigenous peoples. Winter settled in, and the explorers made camp, waiting patiently for the arrival of spring.

When the last snow melted, Coronado pushed on across the plains of Colorado. However, instead of finding golden civilizations, they discovered endless herds of buffalo. Angered by this realization, Coronado confronted El Turco, who then confessed to deceiving them all, spinning tales of El Dorado to gain favor and advance his status. In a fit of rage, Tyrone Sani took matters into his own hands and ended El Turco's life. Tyrone dumped him in the wilderness, leaving his body for the coyotes.

With their dreams of great wealth shattered, Coronado and his ill-fated expedition retreated to the Rio Grande and New Spain. The promise of hidden gold and silver in these lands remained. However, centuries would pass before intrepid prospectors would pry it from the ground.

Unlike his fellow adventurers, Tyrone Sani did not return south. Instead, he journeyed back to the smallPueblo, where he had spent the winter. It was there that he had fallen deeply in love with Tahoma, the daughter of the tribal shaman, whose beauty could rival the radiance of the sun. Tahoma had a goodness that could melt even the coldest heart. Tyrone, a powerful shape-shifting god, was not immune to her charms.

However, Tahoma's loving father disapproved of their union. He sensed an imbalance in Tyrone's spirit, his Chindi, and distrusted the conquistador, who had no ancestral clan. Nevertheless, they were married in a traditional ceremony, with a sacred wedding basket placed nearby to bless the bond. They positioned the basket facing east to catch the blessings of the rising sun each day.

Tyrone embraced his new role as a hunter and settled into the rhythm of everyday life. But beneath the happiness he shared with Tahoma, something stirred within him. He longed to return to his quest for the Izbek crystals, seeking salvation, rescue, and a return to the grandeur of his past life on his home world - to swim again in the communal oceans. The parched land and the monotony of Pueblo life wearied him.

One stormy night, with the full moon trying to break through the clouds, tragedy struck. Insects chirped and reveled in the water droplets left clinging to the grass by the rain. Everything seemed tranquil and normal as a slight breeze promised plenty.

However, screams of agony and despair pierced the night, awakening the entire village. Tahoma, soaked with sweat and blood, lay on the ground, a beautifully woven Navajo blanket stained with the evidence of her pain. Desperately praying to her ancestors, she pleaded with them to save her life.

Amidst the chaos, the tribe's women and the revered shaman scrambled to save the mother and child. They chanted ancient incantations, their voices reaching a crescendo as they prayed to the spirits for mercy. Despite their efforts, the life of the beautiful Navajo princess slipped away. As her spirit left, she gave birth to a stillborn and grotesquely deformed child.

Whispers spread through the village like untamed wildfire. Tales spun of a black raven, a harbinger of darkness, visiting the newlyweds' home. Accompanying the bird was the coyote, an evil spirit known as Ma'ii, who slunk away into the desert, leaving a trail of sorrow.

Tyrone Sani vanished without a trace, with many believing that he had followed behind the coyote, drawn deeper into the darkness that infested his soul.

Burdened by guilt, the shaman regretted the day Tyrone Sani, the conquistador, had come to their village. His arrival stole their innocence, and a dormant evil awakened. The Yee Naaldooshi, known as the feared skin-walker, now haunted the land, bringing death and misery to the Navajo people.

STORY THIRTEEN.

THE WENDIGO.

Passage One

The Legend.

Deep within the cold, primordial forest and the Algonquin people's consciousness lives the Wendigo: a towering, emaciated being with translucent skin draped over its skeletal frame like a veil of mortality. Its hollow eyes gleam like fiery coals, emanating a malevolent crimson glow that mirrors its unquenchable craving for human flesh. Banished from its celestial abode by wrathful sky deities, the Wendigo descended to earth during a turbulent tempest, enshrouded within a colossal silver raindrop.

Passage Two. The Hunt.

Wapun's apprehension had transcended mere fear; he was terrified. "Without fear, there can be no bravery," his grandfather had told him, and he wanted to make him proud. Determined not to return to the village empty-handed from his first solo hunt, at the age of sixteen, he understood this was his chance to prove his manhood - a rite of passage for a young Algonquin brave.

Adorned with sacred markings, he bore the weight of generations past on his sinew-laden limbs. Whispers, reminiscent of forgotten lullabies, echoed through his veins, enveloping him in an unsettling chill of uncertainty. The forest, a crucible of life and death, pulsated with a vitality that both beckoned and repelled.

The autumn trees had thinned, exuding a dark, foreboding presence while the promise of winter wafted upward from the decaying piles of leaves. Bears had not yet gone to their dens to hibernate and would be actively seeking food to fatten up before winter. He would make a nice meal for a ravenous grizzly, cougar, or the packs of wolves that ran along the north ridge.

Armed with a bone knife, a gleaming tomahawk passed down by his grandfather, and a quiver full of arrows, he felt a sense of readiness. His modest yet sturdy bow boasted fine craftsmanship, his skill as a sharpshooter unwavering. Amidst the untamed realm where both majestic and savage beasts lurked, it was not just the physical entities that sent shivers down his spine. Legends whispered of an evil spirit, its malevolence seeking chaos and despair within these haunted woods.

The village elders spun campfire stories of young warriors who ventured into the great forest, never to return; only to be transformed into flesh-eating demons upon meeting the Wendigo. He fervently hoped the deer tracks that he was following would lead him to his prey, allowing him to make a clean kill, return home, and escape these cursed woods.

In a lifetime, he would venture into these woods alone just once, a tradition respected by his mother who silently beseeched her ancestors for his safe return.

Tracking the deer prints to the river where they veered uphill to an area with fewer trees, he noticed another set of unusual tracks - those of a four-legged creature bearing a peculiar U-shaped footprint, unmistakably the mark of a horse with iron shoes. The notion of abandoning the deer hunt for fresher tracks briefly crossed his mind.

However, he was suddenly frozen in place by the otherworldly sound of an animal in pain. While catching his breath, a massive form charged him at full speed, its snorting nostrils and wide eyes betraying its desperate intent to escape. Knocked to the ground with force as the horse dashed past, he glimpsed the fear etched in its eyes, the deep wounds along its flanks, and the telltale U.S. Cavalry markings on its scattered blanket and saddle.

A haunting cry of anguish pierced the air once more, echoing a savage roar saturated with primal gratification. Drawing his bow with haste, he nocked an arrow and ascended the hill cautiously, pausing at the crest to confront a sight that filled him with dread.

On the ground lay a three-hundred-pound buck, still alive but barely, with impressive antlers. Standing over it and devouring its flesh was his grandfather's demon. Suddenly, the monster reared up, its skinny, ugly, gaunt form now standing ten feet tall, with remnants of flesh and blood cascading from its mouth. It turned its head towards him and growled. The young hunter released his arrow, grabbed a piece of the blood-soaked clothing, and fled.

Tumbling down the hill at breakneck speed, his trembling limbs stumbled across the river, breath ragged and frantic, haunted by the echoes of the Wendigo's menacing roar. His heart raced, a drumbeat of sheer adrenaline pulsating through his veins, propelling him forward. Leaping over fallen branches and gnarled roots with the agility of a startled deer, he yearned for the safety of his village, seeking solace in the embrace of his mother who had nurtured him with wisdom and love.

Through the dense thicket, a glimmer of light beckoned, revealing an open meadow basking in the golden rays of sunshine. With a final surge of determination, the young brave burst out of the trees towards the sanctuary. Arriving in the open clearing, his legs buckled beneath him, hands trembling as they touched the soft earth, grounding him in the comforting reality of safety. Gasping for air, chest heaving with gratitude, he looked up at the sky, inhaling the sweet scent of freedom carried by the autumn breeze.

The woods, the river, and that terrible scene of carnage were left far behind in the distance. Wapun stared down at the blood-soaked clothing, his only trophy to celebrate his bravery, and contemplated the soldier's unthinkable fate.

Passage Three.

Solitude.

If one ventures east from the bustling city of Seattle, traversing the meandering Skagit River, an encounter with nature's embrace in the form of the magnificent Cascade Mountains awaits. A twenty-mile boat ride up Lake Ross from the one-horse town of Marblemount leaves you surrounded by verdant woodlands, gazing up at the majestic peaks.

From there, the climb is tough on paths littered with discarded pine needles. The trail continues upward under the sheltering canopy of giant red cedars and Ponderosa pines. The majestic trees reach skyward with grace, their trunks so wide that it would take thirty people, linking arms, to encircle them. Humble beneath their towering presence, the Pacific silver firs appear as mere ankle biters in comparison.

However, amidst the harmony of the forest, a man of duality named Daemon Abbadon lives in this wondrous place. When called upon, he acts as a contract killer for the Sobek corporation, but daily, he dons a different guise, taking on the role of smoke spotter. He stands guard against the dangerous threat of fire for the forestry service.

Within the solace of a lonely cabin, perched loftily upon the aptly named Desolation Peak, this enigmatic figure leads a solitary existence, untouched by the pulsating beat of urban life. Every day, he awakens to a tapestry of splendor, cast in the gentle morning glow, while the very essence of the untamed woods - fragrant and ethereal- dances upon the lips of a fresh mountain breeze.

Passage Four.

The Monster.

Daemon had arrived on this planet many moons ago, separated from his fellow Izbek castaways by a vast continent and an impenetrable ocean. Unfortunately, his landing was far from routine, with his sphere malfunctioning and colliding with an enormous tree. It left him with a ghastly wound that spanned from his forehead to the nape of his neck. Though he applied a living liquid, replete with microscopic machines designed to mend and sustain his body, his brain suffered an irreparable trauma. Despite the nanites dutifully tending to the damage, a loss of mental agility was inevitable. Unsure of how to continue, Daemon clung to his magical amulet for countless days, telepathically straining to contact any fellow survivors.

Upon descent, Daemon noted at least one other sphere navigating the planet's atmosphere. He felt sure it had landed on this continent, yet his requests returned only silence. His peers had not survived their crash landing or were too far away to respond. Moreover, the Izbek mother ship had left orbit to return home, leaving no way of relaying any message.

Finally, Daemon realized his lonely situation, accepting that he was alone and would need to adapt to this new world.

Daemon chanced upon a small group of primordial humans in the depths of a river valley.

Living in rudimentary shelters fashioned from animal pelts, they subsisted by hunting large herds of woolly creatures and foraging in the densely forested hills.

Daemon recognized an opportunity to mold himself to this alien world, opting to assimilate into this tribe's form for his everyday life. In these primitive humans, he discovered a semblance of comfort and companionship.

To both hunt and survive, Daemon chose various creatures as his avatars, assuming the identities of the fearsome dire wolf, the agile smilodon, and the formidable short-faced bear. Initially, he could transform into any of these prehistoric beasts. But a combination of his existing disability and the onset of a debilitating bone disease common among wolves and saber-toothed cats curtailed his transformative powers.

Daemon's ability to shift became confused. Instead of appearing as one of these fearsome creatures, he transformed into a ghoulish combination of all three. Moreover, the animal's frantic multiple personalities turned him berserk with uncontrollable rage. Reduced to an insanely hideous monster, he survived by eating men, the simplest of prey to catch.

Continuously muttering strange words into his amulet, Daemon withdrew from social interaction. Fearing he was insane and a danger to their children, the elders banished Daemon from the tribe. Alone once again, he found refuge in the wooded mountains, where he struggled to survive. He only ate when unsuspecting victims crossed his path, or hunger forced him into the valley to prey on his former people.

The tribal shaman, complicit in its evolution, passed down campfire stories of the Wendigo, a human-bear demon that roamed the forests, walked upright, and relished the taste of human flesh.

Daemon survived countless frozen winters before he finally sensed the presence of some of his former shipmates. In the 16th century, some of the Izbek had finally come west and north onto this frontier, traveling alongside Spanish conquistadors, French trappers, and English settlers who sought riches and a new way of life.

However, Daemon, estranged by his prolonged isolation, hesitated to initiate contact. He finally broke his silence when Sobek a fellow castaway arrived in the bustling port of New Bedford, Massachusetts. Sobek, now known as Martin Krugler, was an investor in the burgeoning whaling industry.

Through his amulet Krugler at once sensed the weight of Daemon's history and his tormented psyche. He understood the Herculean task of reintegrating his fellow Izbek into the fabric of society. Nonetheless, Krugler had found a potential instrument for his dark designs and extended a hand to the enigmatic outcast, rescuing him from his hermitic life.

Krugler dispatched the captain of the Minerva, one of his whaling ships that exploited the cetacean-rich waters of Alaska. They were to retrieve a solitary human on the west coast of Washington state once their barrels were brimming with precious whale oil.

As the Minerva steered a course back to the civilized shores of New England, an unsettling wave of misfortune washed over the ship. When they received this strange and unusual passenger, the crew wondered if an ill omen had come onboard. Tempestuous storms claimed the lives of three experienced sailors, swallowed by the raging seas as they stood their watch.

Wherever Daemon Abbadon, the fearsome Wendigo, traveled, men vanished without a trace. He was the embodiment of the archetypal serial killer. This insidious predator became a phantom suspect, forever eluding his pursuers. Devouring his victims without leaving clues, he relinquished trophies in favor of consuming their every bone - a macabre feast akin to a dutiful child licking his plate clean.

Upon the Minerva's arrival in New Bedford, Krugler looked to reintroduce Daemon into the complexities of urban life. Yet, the creature of the wilderness found no comfort in the city despite the bountiful opportunities to prey upon those in need and the vulnerable. Therefore, with the advent of the railroads, Daemon abandoned the East Coast and returned to the mountains of his ancestral home, never losing his unquenchable appetite for human flesh.

Passage Five.

The Serial Killer.

When an escape pod once thought lost appeared in the United States, Krugler was awash with excitement. The extraterrestrial contents within would certainly prolong his domination over world commerce.

Krugler dispatched Daemon to Lake Mead to be part of the recovery team and to join a group of mercenaries paid for by the corporation.

"You never know when you might have use of a stone-cold Killer" Krugler mused.

Daemon reluctantly left behind his ancestral hunting grounds and perch on top of Desolation Peak. It was mid-October, marking the end of the wildfire season. The recent heavy rainfall in the northwest had minimized the risk of fire in the sodden timbers below his cabin. Therefore, Daemon felt certain that he would not be missed.

Retrieving his pickup truck from beside the Marblemount community club, Daemon planned to take Interstate eighty two and eighty four through Idaho, eventually driving down US Route ninety three into Vegas. With necessary rest stops factored in, the arduous journey would take approximately two days.

As darkness fell, exhaustion and hunger nipped at Daemon's heels, prompting the decision to spend the night at the humble Motel six in Twin Falls, Idaho. Intent on an early start the following morning, he hoped to reach the shores of the lake by nightfall.

Twin Falls, because of its harsh winters, had not a significant homeless population. However, Old Ned Taylor, the local drunk, sought shelter nightly, despite Kevin Phillips, the no-nonsense motel manager constantly chasing him away. Ned had often talked of escaping the cold by moving to California, but those plans had never come to fruition. However, concern arose when a bartender at the Bucket of Suds saloon mentioned that no one had seen Ned in days.

Curiosity piqued, Kevin followed the advice of his landscapers and searched the motel property. Grim evidence of Ned's presence greeted him - empty rum bottles, a torn sleeping bag, and makeshift cardboard flooring beneath a broken patio umbrella. The stench of urine, alcohol, and body odor lingered, mingling with old rags and discarded food wrappers, stinging Kevin's nose. The sight of a cold fire in a makeshift hearth, constructed from a metal oil drum, hinted at abandonment. Had Ned finally made it to California or succumbed to a drunken stupor and fallen off the Perrine Memorial Bridge into the icy Snake River?

Anticipating Ned's inevitable return, Kevin nevertheless instructed his crew to clean up the area. However, days turned into weeks, and still, Ned remained absent. A sense of unease and sadness settled over the motel. Wherever Daemon Abbadon, the enigmatic Wendigo, wandered, people vanished without a trace.

Arriving at the lake, the team of mercenaries met Daemon's presence with skepticism. With no military background and only forestry service experience, he claimed to be proficient with a rifle, but doubts lingered. His withdrawn nature and intense gaze unsettled the soldiers, as if he were watching them, evaluating their worth. It reminded them of a ravenous animal or combat veteran yearning for the adrenaline of battle. This type of person was always on edge and agitated, as if experiencing withdrawals from an out-of-reach drug.

Krugler's team consisted of professional soldiers who relied on each other for support. They could not afford any distractions or a team member who could not keep control, for it would spell disaster.

Krugler however, assured them of

Daemon's importance to their operation. Their trusted leaders' words held weight. Yet the soldiers could not help but wonder if this time would be different. Would Daemon Abbadon disappoint or prove them wrong for doubting him? Only time would tell.

The day after Daemon arrived, Joey Rogan, a former Navy SEAL, went missing. The group looked to Daemon for answers, but just like the desert wind blowing across the lake, he too had disappeared.

Wherever Daemon Abbadon, the enigmatic Wendigo, wandered, people vanished without a trace.

The End.

I dedicate this book to my mother who inspired a generation of Yorkshire women.

About the Author.

R.M. Alwyn is a writer living in Southern California. Born in Huddersfield, Yorkshire in the United Kingdom, R.M attended King James School in Almondbury and the University of Manchester. He graduated with honors before emigrating to the United States. He authored his trilogy of books initially for his children before deciding to publish them.

He writes not only to entertain but also to educate and inspire readers to investigate the world we live in, its history, and the fantastic stories told in many of its cultures.

A Humble Request.

I am truly touched by your decision to read or listen to my book. Your support means the world to me and fuels my passion for writing, allowing me to delve into creating more captivating stories. If you could kindly consider leaving an honest online review of my book at the platform where you made your purchase, it would mean everything to me. Your feedback holds immense value, as it guides bookstores in deciding how to further distribute and promote my work. Your time and attention devoted to reading my book fill me with gratitude, and I genuinely hope that it brought you as much joy as it brought me while I poured my heart into it.

Books published.

The Descendants of Gods Trilogy.
https://www.amazon.com/dp/B0CZLW2QBP
Raindrops of the Gods.
Jewels beneath the Loch.
Retribution of Fire.

Meet The Author And Find Out What is New in The Cosmos.

Website:
https://quadsquadauthor.com

www.ingramcontent.com/pod-product-compliance
Lightning Source LLC
Chambersburg PA
CBHW010133150626
46552CB00023B/3224